NORSE MYTHOLOGY UNLEASHED

DISCOVER THE ORIGIN OF VIKING TRADITIONS, GODS AND GODDESSES, AND MYTHICAL CREATURES ON A JOURNEY THROUGH NORSE PAGANISM

ANTHONY POE

CONTENTS

INTRODUCTION

Have you ever wondered how the myths that shaped the Vikings' worldview continue to resonate in our modern world? How do stories of gods and giants, heroic deeds, and epic battles still find their way into our books, movies, and even video games? These ancient tales, woven from the threads of Norse mythology, are as captivating today as they were in the halls of ancient Scandinavia.

Norse mythology is a rich collection of stories that include gods and goddesses like Odin and Freyja, heroes like Sigurd, mythical creatures like the fearsome Fenrir, and the powerful runes that hold deep magical significance. It is a world where the mighty Thor battles giants with his hammer, Mjölnir, the trickster Loki weaves his schemes, and the majestic Yggdrasil, the World Tree, connects the realms of gods, humans, and the dead. Beyond entertainment, these stories were a vital part of the Norse people's culture and worldview, shaping their understanding of life, death, and the cosmos.

This book aims to provide you, the reader, with a comprehensive yet accessible guide to Norse mythology. Whether you are a curious beginner or looking to deepen your knowledge, this book aims to make the complex world of Norse myths understandable and fascinating. We will explore the history and creation of these myths, explore the roles of various deities and mythical beings, and uncover the cultural significance they held for the Vikings.

The book is structured to take you on a journey through the many layers of Norse mythology. We will start with the origins of these myths, exploring how they were passed down through oral tradition and eventually written down in texts like the Poetic Edda and the Prose Edda. Then, we will dive into detailed profiles of gods and goddesses, legendary heroes, and mythical creatures. We will examine key myths and legends, rituals and symbols, and finally, we will look at the enduring impact of Norse mythology on modern culture.

Why is Norse mythology still important today? These ancient stories continue to inspire and captivate us. They appear in literature, movies, TV shows, and video games, influencing everything from J.R.R. Tolkien's Middle-earth to the Marvel Universe's portrayal of Thor and Loki. Modern paganism draws heavily from these myths, and they remain a source of fascination for many who seek to understand the beliefs and values of ancient societies. The timeless nature of these stories, with their themes of bravery, betrayal, love, and sacrifice, speaks to the human condition in ways that are still relevant today.

Allow me to share a personal note. My name is Anthony Poe, and my passion for world mythology began in my youth. Hearing stories of heroes, legends, and gods transported me to a world of wonder and adventure. This fascination grew with time as I decided to pursue and study mythology and ancient cultures, dedicating my life to understanding and sharing these incredible tales.

This book is the culmination of my lifelong passion, and I hope it will ignite a similar spark of curiosity and wonder in you.

As you read this book, you can expect to gain a deeper understanding of Norse myths. You will learn to recognize their influences on modern culture and appreciate the timeless nature of these stories. Each chapter is designed to be engaging and enlightening, combining historical facts with captivating narratives to bring the world of Norse mythology to life.

So, dear reader, I invite you to embark on this journey through the realms of Norse mythology. Together, we will traverse the nine worlds, meet gods and giants, and uncover the secrets of runes and rituals. Prepare to be enthralled by tales of heroism, trickery, creation, and destruction and discover the enduring power of these ancient stories. The adventure awaits.

1

THE DAWN OF NORSE MYTHOLOGY

Have you ever pondered the origins of the universe through the lens of ancient Norse beliefs? How did the cosmos, with its intricate realms and formidable beings, come into existence according to the Vikings? In the vast expanse of Norse mythology, the story of creation begins with a yawning void, an endless chasm that predates everything. This chapter explores the primordial chaos and birth of the cosmos, setting the stage for the gods, giants, and humans who inhabit these timeless tales.

GINNUNGAGAP AND THE BIRTH OF THE COSMOS

At the heart of Norse cosmology lies Ginnungagap, an immense void that existed before the dawn of time. It is the primordial emptiness, a boundless abyss that separates the fiery realm of Muspelheim from the icy wasteland of Niflheim. Unlike the Greek concept of Chaos, which also represents a formless void, Ginnungagap is the canvas upon which the Norse cosmos was painted. It is both nothingness and the potential for everything, a vast expanse that holds the seeds of creation.

To the north of Ginnungagap lay Niflheim, a realm shrouded in ice and mist. This desolate land was home to rivers of venom and glaciers, its frigid landscape a stark contrast to the fiery domain of Muspelheim to the south. Muspelheim, on the other hand, was a realm of unending fire and searing heat, guarded by the fearsome giant Surtr. With his flaming sword, Surtr stood watch over this blazing world, ready to unleash its destructive power at the end of days.

The interaction between these two opposing realms within Ginnungagap set the stage for the creation of the cosmos. As the icy rivers from Niflheim flowed into the void, they met the sparks and molten matter from Muspelheim. The intense heat caused the ice to melt, and from these primordial waters emerged Ymir, the first being. Ymir was a giant, a creature born from the union of fire and ice. His existence was the beginning of life within the void, a bridge between the realms of ice and flame.

Alongside Ymir, another being emerged from the melting ice: the cow Audhumla. Audhumla played an important role in nourishing Ymir and providing the sustenance he needed to thrive. As Audhumla licked the salty ice blocks, she uncovered Buri, the ancestor of the gods. This act of creation from the ice and the birth of beings like Ymir and Audhumla highlight the dynamic interplay between the elements within Ginnungagap.

Ginnungagap's significance in Norse cosmology extends beyond its role as the birthplace of life. It represents the delicate balance between creation and destruction, a theme that recurs throughout Norse myths. The void is a realm of potential where the forces of fire and ice continuously interact to shape existence. This concept of balance is central to the Norse understanding of the world, where creation often emerges from chaos and order from disorder.

Understanding Ginnungagap and its role in the birth of the cosmos provides a foundation for exploring the rich tapestry of Norse mythology. It is the starting point from which the gods, giants, and other beings emerge, each playing their part in the grand narrative of the Norse cosmos. As we dive deeper into these myths, the significance of Ginnungagap will become apparent, offering insights into the worldview of the ancient Norse people.

YMIR'S SACRIFICE AND THE FORMATION OF THE WORLDS

Ymir, the first of the giants, sprang to life from the melting ice of Ginnungagap, a being defined by his enormous stature and primal power. As he slumbered, the sweat from his body gave birth to other giants, marking the beginning of a lineage that would play a key role in Norse cosmology. A male and female giant emerged from his armpits and another from his legs. These beings would populate the world with the Jotunn, the race of giants who would often stand in opposition to the gods.

Ymir's existence, however, was not eternal. His life ended in a cataclysmic event orchestrated by Odin and his brothers, Vili and Vé. The three gods, seeking to bring order to the cosmos, decided that Ymir's body would be the foundation of a new world. Ymir's body was dismembered, and each part was used to craft the elements of the universe. From his flesh, they formed the earth, a solid ground for life to flourish. His blood flowed to create the seas, vast and deep, teeming with potential. The mountains emerged from his bones, standing as eternal sentinels over the land. Ymir's skull was lifted to form the sky, held aloft by four dwarves named Norðri, Suðri, Austri, and Vestri, who represented the cardinal directions. His brain became the clouds drifting across the heavens.

Odin, Vili, and Vé were the architects of the cosmos. Their role in Ymir's sacrifice was pivotal, as they transformed chaos into order. Odin, the eldest, was known for his wisdom and foresight, qualities that were instrumental in the creation process. Vili, whose name means "will," embodied the determination and resolve necessary to bring about such a monumental change. Vé, whose name signifies "sanctuary" or "holy," represented the sacred nature of their task. Together, they shaped the world from Ymir's remains, setting the stage for the existence of gods, giants, and humans alike.

Ymir's sacrifice is a key theme in Norse mythology, representing the cycle of creation and destruction. His death gave birth to the cosmos, reflecting the belief that violence and endings often lead to new beginnings. This idea echoes in the prophecy of Ragnarok, where the world's end paves the way for its rebirth, continuing the cosmic cycle.

In addition, Ymir's dismemberment symbolizes transformation, as his body formed the world. This mirrors the natural cycle of death and renewal, where one season's end brings another's start. His sacrifice reflects the Norse view that change and regeneration are essential to life. His legacy is woven into the fabric of the Norse cosmos—the earth, sea, sky, and mountains are all reminders of his foundational act. His story illustrates the interconnectedness of all beings—giants, gods, and humans—bound together in a shared destiny from the moment he emerged from the ice.

THE NINE REALMS OF YGGDRASIL

Yggdrasil, the World Tree, stands at the heart of Norse cosmology. This immense ash tree is a vital structure that holds the fabric of the universe together. Its branches stretch out into the heavens, while its roots go deep into the underworld, connecting the nine realms of the Norse cosmos. Yggdrasil's central role is the axis mundi, the cosmic axis around which everything revolves. Each realm is anchored by its roots or touched by its branches, symbolizing the interconnected nature of all existence within Norse mythology.

Asgard, perched high among Yggdrasil's branches, is the realm of the Aesir gods. This is where Odin, Thor, and their kin reside, governing the universe from their celestial stronghold. Asgard is often depicted as a shining city of golden halls and mighty fortresses, a place of great power and wisdom. Here, the gods hold a council, plan their strategies against the giants, and prepare for the prophesied events of Ragnarok.

Midgard, the realm of humans, lies in the middle of Yggdrasil's structure. It is our world, a place of both beauty and hardship, where people live their lives unaware of the grand cosmic battles that take place above and below. Midgard is connected to Asgard by the Bifrost, the rainbow bridge that allows gods to travel to and from the human world. This connection signifies the close yet complex relationship between gods and men.

Jotunheim, the land of the giants, is a realm of rugged landscapes and untamed wilderness. Giants, or Jotunn, inhabit this realm, constantly clashing with the gods in their quest for dominance. Jotunheim is characterized by its harsh environment, filled with towering mountains and deep forests, reflecting the formidable nature of its inhabitants.

Alfheim, the realm of the light elves, is a place of ethereal beauty and tranquility. Light elves, known for their wisdom and grace, dwell here, often aiding gods and humans with their knowledge. Alfheim is a realm filled with light and magic, starkly contrasting the darker realms within Yggdrasil.

Svartalfheim, the home of the dwarves, lies deep within the earth. Dwarves are master craftsmen known for creating some of the most powerful artifacts in Norse mythology, including Thor's hammer Mjölnir. Svartalfheim is a realm of subterranean forges and mines where these industrious beings work tirelessly.

Vanaheim, the land of the Vanir gods, is another celestial realm within Yggdrasil. The Vanir are associated with nature, fertility, and prosperity. Their realm is lush and abundant, reflecting the aspects they govern. The Vanir gods, including Freyr and Freyja, once waged war against the Aesir but later formed a truce, signifying the unity and balance within the cosmos.

Niflheim, a realm of ice and mist, is one of the primordial realms within Yggdrasil. It is a place of cold and desolation, home to the frost giants and the dragon Nidhogg. Niflheim's icy rivers and glaciers are a stark reminder of the harsh and unforgiving aspects of nature.

Muspelheim, the fiery counterpart to Niflheim, is a realm of fire and heat. Guarded by the giant Surtr, Muspelheim is a land of molten lava and perpetual flames. This realm represents the destructive forces of the cosmos, always in tension with the icy desolation of Niflheim.

Helheim, the underworld, is ruled by Hel, Loki's daughter. It is where the souls of those who did not die in battle reside, a place of shadow and reflection. Helheim is not a realm of torment but a somber abode for the dead, emphasizing the Norse belief in the cyclical nature of life and death.

Yggdrasil's roots and branches play a role in connecting these realms. The roots extend into various parts of the cosmos, anchoring the tree and drawing sustenance from the wells of wisdom and fate. One of the most important wells is the Well of Urd, where the Norns—three powerful beings who control fate—reside. These roots are also gnawed at by Nidhogg, a serpent that symbolizes the ever-present threat of decay and destruction.

The branches of Yggdrasil touch each realm, providing a pathway for gods, giants, and other beings to traverse the cosmos. This interconnectedness is central to Norse mythology, illustrating the idea that all realms and beings are part of a greater whole. The tree's existence underscores the continuity of life and death, the balance of opposing forces, and the eternal cycle of creation and destruction.

In Ragnarok's prophecy, Yggdrasil plays a significant role. The tree is shaken to its roots, symbolizing the upheaval and renewal that comes with the end of one world and the beginning of another. Even in this cataclysmic event, Yggdrasil endures, representing the resilience and continuity of life.

AESIR AND VANIR: THE TWO PANTHEONS OF NORSE GODS

In the world of Norse mythology, the deities are divided into two primary pantheons: the Aesir and the Vanir. The Aesir are primarily associated with war, governance, and the overarching order of the cosmos. They reside in Asgard, the realm of the gods, and include powerful figures such as Odin, Thor, and Tyr. Odin, often referred to as the Allfather, is the chief of the Aesir, known for his wisdom, quest for knowledge, and role as a war god. Thor, with his mighty hammer Mjölnir, is the god of thunder and a fierce protector of both gods and humans. Tyr, the one-handed god, embodies justice and valor, often stepping forward in times of conflict to uphold divine law.

On the other hand, the Vanir are closely linked to fertility, prosperity, and the natural world. They dwell in Vanaheim, a realm abundant with life and growth. The Vanir include gods like Freyr, Freyja, and Njord, who bring fertility to the land and seas. Freyr, a god of sunlight and rain, ensures bountiful harvests and is deeply revered for his life-giving powers. Freyja, a goddess of love, beauty, and war, has a multifaceted nature that makes her one of the most beloved deities. Njord, the god of the sea, brings wealth and prosperity through his control over the ocean's bounty.

The relationship between the Aesir and Vanir was not always harmonious. The Aesir-Vanir War, one of the most significant conflicts in Norse mythology, began due to mutual distrust and the desire for supremacy. The war erupted from a series of misunderstandings and acts of aggression, such as the Aesir's suspicion toward the Vanir's magical practices. The conflict raged on for years, resulting in significant losses on both sides. However, the war concluded with reconciliation. As a gesture of peace, the two pantheons exchanged hostages: the Vanir sent Freyr, Freyja, and Njord to live among the Aesir, while the Aesir sent Hoenir and Mimir to reside with the Vanir. This exchange of gods symbolized a truce and the beginning of cooperation between the two groups.

The significance of the unity between the Aesir and Vanir extends beyond just political alliance. It represents the integration of different aspects of life, embodying the harmony between order and nature, war and fertility. The Vanir's integration into Asgard brought a balance essential for the well-being of the cosmos. Freyr and Freyja's presence in Asgard introduced elements of fertility and love, enriching the Aesir's martial and administrative focus. This unity also highlights the Norse belief in balance and coopera-tion, even among powerful rival forces.

Among the Aesir, Odin is a central figure, revered for his wisdom and leadership. Known for his sacrifice to gain the knowledge of runes, Odin is a god who seeks understanding at any cost. Thor, with his thunderous presence, is the defender of gods and humans alike, battling giants and ensuring the safety of the realms. Tyr, often depicted with one hand, sacrificed his limb to bind the monstrous wolf Fenrir, demonstrating his unwavering commitment to justice.

From the Vanir, Freyr is celebrated for his ability to bring fertility and peace. With his magical ship Skidbladnir and his boar Gullinbursti, Freyr commands both land and sea. Freyja, his sister, is a goddess of many facets, revered for her beauty and feared for her warrior spirit. She rides a chariot pulled by cats and weeps tears of gold, embodying both love and sorrow. Njord, their father, oversees the seas and is invoked by sailors and fishermen for safe passage and abundant catches.

The blending of the Aesir and Vanir pantheons enriches the Norse mythological landscape, offering a complex interplay of power, wisdom, love, and fertility. This union is a testament to the Norse understanding of the world's interconnectedness and the necessity of balance in maintaining cosmic order. The stories of these gods continue to captivate and inspire, reflecting the values and beliefs of the ancient Norse people.

CREATION OF THE FIRST HUMANS: ASK AND EMBLA

In the rich landscape of Norse mythology, the creation of the first humans stands as a tale of divine craftsmanship and the infusion of life. The gods Odin, Vili, and Vé, after shaping the cosmos from the body of Ymir, turned their attention to creating beings who could inhabit Midgard, the realm of humans. Their search led them to the seashore, where they found two tree trunks lying side by side—one an ash tree, the other an elm. These lifeless, wooden forms held the potential for something greater. The gods, recognizing this potential, decided to breathe life into them.

Odin, the Allfather, was the first to act. He gave them breath and life, imbuing the wooden figures with the essence of vitality. Vili, whose name signifies will and consciousness, granted them intelligence and movement, enabling them to think and interact with the world around them. Vé, whose name means sacredness, bestowed upon them their senses, emotions, and outward appearance. Through this divine intervention, the ash tree became Ask, the first man, and the elm tree transformed into Embla, the first woman. Together, they embodied the divine gifts of life, intellect, and spirit.

Beyond a story of divine craftsmanship, Ask and Embla's creation holds deep symbolic meaning within Norse mythology. The choice of trees as the material for creating humans highlights the Norse people's connection to nature. Trees, with their roots deep in the earth and branches reaching toward the sky, symbolize the link between the terrestrial and the divine. By turning trees into humans, the gods underscored humanity's intrinsic bond with the natural world. The gifts of breath, intelligence, and senses granted by the gods signify the holistic nature of human existence, where life, thought, and emotion are intertwined.

The story of Ask and Embla finds parallels in other creation myths worldwide. In the Abrahamic traditions, Adam and Eve are fashioned by God and placed in the Garden of Eden, representing the first humans and the beginning of human history. Similarly, Ask and Embla are the progenitors of the human race in Norse mythology. Both stories emphasize the divine origin of humanity and the special relationship between humans and their creators. In various Indo-European myths, we find similar themes where gods create humans from natural elements like clay, wood, or stone, further highlighting the universal motif of divine creation.

In the grand narrative of Norse mythology, the creation of Ask and Embla marks the beginning of human history. Their story, woven with divine intervention and natural symbolism, offers insights into the Norse worldview. As we examine these myths, we uncover layers of meaning that continue to resonate with us, bridging the gap between ancient wisdom and modern understanding.

2

THE PANTHEON OF GODS AND GODDESSES

What makes a god worthy of reverence? Is it wisdom, bravery, or perhaps the willingness to sacrifice for the greater good? In Norse mythology, Odin, the Allfather, embodies all these traits and more. As the king of the Aesir gods, Odin's influence stretches across the realms, intertwining wisdom, war, and the mysteries of life and death.

ODIN THE ALLFATHER: WISDOM, WAR, AND SACRIFICE

Odin's relentless quest for wisdom is a cornerstone of his character. Unlike other deities who might inherit their knowledge, Odin earned his through significant sacrifices. One of the most striking examples is his encounter with Mimir's well. Mimir, the guardian of the well, possessed unparalleled wisdom, and Odin desired to drink from its waters. However, the price was steep: Mimir demanded one of Odin's eyes in exchange. Without hesitation, Odin plucked out his eye and cast it into the well, gaining the wisdom he sought but forever bearing the mark of his sacrifice—a single, all-seeing eye that missed nothing.

This wasn't the only time Odin sacrificed part of himself for knowledge. In a harrowing display of dedication, he hanged himself from Yggdrasil, the World Tree, for nine days and nights. Speared and suffering, Odin hung between life and death, seeking the secrets of the runes. These ancient symbols held great power and wisdom, capable of magic and prophecy. Through his ordeal, Odin learned the runes and became a master of their use, adding another layer to his vast reservoir of knowledge. This act of self-sacrifice underscores Odin's relentless pursuit of understanding, a commitment to wisdom that few can match.

Odin's role as a war god is equally significant. His connection to battle is deeply practical and strategic. Odin oversees the selection of the Einherjar, the fallen warriors chosen by Valkyries to reside in Valhalla. These warriors are the bravest and most skilled souls, destined to fight alongside the gods during Ragnarok, the end of the world. Odin's presence on the battlefield is said to influence the outcome of wars, offering victory to those he favors and ensuring that worthy warriors join his ranks in Valhalla. This connection to war highlights Odin's dual nature as a wise leader and a fierce warrior, embodying the qualities of both a sage and a general.

Odin's attributes and symbols are rich with meaning, each telling a story of its own. His spear, Gungnir, is a weapon of unparalleled accuracy, said to never miss its mark. This symbol of precision and power reflects Odin's strategic mind and unerring judgment. His ravens, Huginn and Muninn, are his eyes and ears, flying across the realms to bring him information. Huginn represents thought, and Muninn represents memory, together embodying the dual aspects of wisdom that Odin values. Sleipnir, his eight-legged horse, is another of his remarkable symbols. This incredible steed, born of Loki's shapeshifting mischief, can travel through all realms, signifying Odin's ability to navigate the universe's complexities. The Valknut, a symbol often associated with Odin, represents his connection to death and the afterlife, reinforcing his role as a god who bridges the living and the dead.

Several key myths highlight Odin's multifaceted nature. One such story is the creation of the world, where Odin and his brothers, Vili and Vé, slew the primordial giant Ymir. From Ymir's body, they fashioned the cosmos, demonstrating Odin's role as a creator and shaper of reality. Another significant tale is Odin's involvement in the Aesir-Vanir War. This conflict between the two pantheons of gods was resolved through Odin's wisdom and diplomacy, leading to a truce that unified the Aesir and Vanir, enriching Asgard with the diversity and strengths of both groups.

These stories and symbols weave together to form a complex portrait of Odin. He is a god who sacrifices for wisdom, leads in battle, and shapes the cosmos with his will. His relentless pursuit of knowledge, strategic mind, and deep connection to the mysteries of life and death make him a central figure in Norse mythology. This deity embodies the values and complexities of the ancient Norse worldview.

FRIGG: THE ALL-MOTHER AND GODDESS OF FATE

Frigg stands as Asgard's queen, Odin's wife, and Baldr's mother. Her presence in the halls of Asgard is one of regality and wisdom, commanding respect from all gods and goddesses. As Odin's consort, Frigg holds a unique position of influence, often acting as a counselor and confidante to her husband. Her domain, the Hall of Fensalir, is a place of warmth and domestic tranquility, reflecting her role as a protector of the home and family. Here, she manages the household's affairs, guiding the other goddesses and ensuring the smooth running of daily life in Asgard. Frigg's influence extends beyond her immediate family; she is a motherly figure to all the Aesir, embodying the values of love, care, and foresight.

Frigg's association with fate and prophecy adds a layer of complexity to her character. She possesses the rare gift of fore-knowledge, allowing her to see events before they unfold. This ability, however, comes with its own set of challenges. One of the most poignant examples of this is her knowledge of her son Baldr's impending death. Despite her foresight, Frigg is bound by the limitations of her power. She cannot alter the course of fate, which adds a tragic dimension to her character. Frigg's decision to remain silent about certain prophecies, including Baldr's death, speaks to her wisdom and restraint. She understands that some knowledge, while valuable, can also be a burden.

Key symbols associated with Frigg further illuminate her role and attributes. The spindle and distaff are her primary symbols, repre-senting her connection to domestic life and her influence over fate. These spinning and weaving tools are metaphors for the threads of destiny that Frigg weaves. Her ability to spin the threads of life, determining the fates of gods and humans alike, under-scores her role as a goddess of fate. In her household, Frigg is served by loyal handmaidens, each with their own distinct roles. Fulla, one of her closest attendants, is entrusted with Frigg's secrets and treasures. The presence of these handmaidens high-lights Frigg's status and the respect she commands within Asgard.

Frigg's influence and attributes paint a picture of a goddess who embodies domesticity and divine power. Her wisdom, foresight, and maternal care make her a revered figure in Norse mythology. Whether she is managing the Hall of Fensalir, foreseeing the future, or weaving the threads of destiny, Frigg's presence is one of grace and strength. Her stories remind us of love's enduring power, fate's inevitability, and the deep impact of a mother's devotion.

THOR: THE THUNDER GOD AND PROTECTOR OF MANKIND

Thor, the mighty god of thunder, is one of the most revered figures in Norse mythology. His role as a protector is multifaceted, encompassing the defense of both gods and humans from a variety of threats. Thor's battles against giants, known as Jotunn, are legendary. These giants, embodiments of chaos and destruction, frequently challenge the order maintained by the gods. Thor, with his immense strength and unyielding courage, often finds himself at the forefront of these conflicts, wielding his iconic hammer, Mjölnir, with devastating effect. Mjölnir is a symbol of Thor's power and commitment to protecting the realms. The hammer's ability to return to Thor's hand after being thrown ensures that no enemy can escape his wrath, no matter how formidable.

Thor's attributes and symbols further enhance his image as a formidable protector. One of the most significant of these is Megingjord, a belt that doubles his already prodigious strength. With Megingjord, Thor's might becomes nearly unparalleled, allowing him to perform feats of strength that would be impossible for any other being. Another key symbol is his chariot, pulled by two goats named Tanngrisnir and Tanngnjóstr. These goats serve as his mode of transport across the skies and reflect his connection to the land and the supernatural. Thor's chariot, often seen streaking through the heavens, is a vivid reminder of his constant vigilance and readiness to defend against any threat.

Thor's personality is as striking as his physical attributes. His bravery is unquestionable; he charges into battles with a straightforward determination that inspires both gods and men. However, this bravery is often accompanied by a quick temper. Thor does not tolerate injustice or deceit, and his reactions can be swift and severe. Yet, this temper is balanced by a strong sense of justice. Thor fights not for personal glory but to maintain the balance and protect the innocent. His actions are guided by a deep moral code, making him a hero in the truest sense.

Several myths highlight Thor's heroic deeds and complex character. One such story is his fishing trip to catch Jormungandr, the Midgard Serpent. Disguised as a fisherman, Thor set out with the giant Hymir to the deepest part of the ocean. Using an ox head as bait, Thor managed to hook Jormungandr. The struggle between Thor and the serpent was monumental, with the force of their battle causing the seas to churn violently. Although the encounter ended with Hymir cutting the line in fear, Thor's bravery in facing such a formidable foe is undeniable.

Another tale is Thor's journey to Utgard-Loki's hall. During this adventure, Thor and his companions face a series of seemingly impossible challenges set by the giant king Utgard-Loki. Despite his immense strength, Thor was humbled by tasks that were revealed to be illusions, such as trying to lift a cat that was actually the Midgard Serpent in disguise. This story showcases Thor's strength and willingness to face humiliation and learn from his experiences.

Another captivating myth is about the theft and retrieval of Mjölnir. When the giant Thrym stole Mjölnir and demanded Freyja's hand in marriage as ransom, Thor devised a clever plan. Disguised as Freyja, with Loki as his handmaiden, Thor infiltrated Thrym's hall. Thor's true identity was revealed during the wedding feast, and he reclaimed Mjölnir, using it to defeat Thrym and his kin. This story highlights Thor's resourcefulness and the deep bond of trust and cooperation he shares with Loki despite their contrasting natures.

Through these myths and symbols, Thor emerges as a true hero yet a relatable figure. His strength and bravery are tempered by moments of vulnerability and humility, making him a god who is both awe-inspiring and deeply human. Thor's unwavering commitment to protecting the realms and his relentless battle against chaos makes him a pillar of Norse mythology and a timeless symbol of heroism.

LOKI: THE TRICKSTER AND CATALYST OF CHANGE

Loki's dual nature makes him one of the most intriguing figures in Norse mythology. He is both a helper and a troublemaker, embodying a complex character that defies simple categorization. On one hand, Loki's cleverness and resourcefulness have aided the gods in numerous situations. His quick thinking and cunning solutions have saved Asgard from various threats, earning him a place among the Aesir despite his Jotunn heritage. On the other hand, Loki's penchant for mischief and chaos often leads to problems that only he can resolve. His actions are unpredictable, swinging between heroism and deceit, making him a figure of both admiration and suspicion.

Loki's attributes and symbols reflect his multifaceted personality. One of his most notable abilities is shapeshifting, allowing him to transform into various forms, from a salmon to a mare. This power symbolizes Loki's fluid identity and knack for adapting to any situation. His association with fire and cunning further underscores his role as a catalyst for change. Fire, like Loki, can be both a source of warmth and a force of destruction. It can forge new paths or reduce everything to ashes, much like Loki's actions in the myths. His cleverness is often likened to the flickering flames, unpredictable and capable of great impact.

Loki's relationships with the other gods are as complex as his character. His friendship with Thor is a perfect example of this intricate dynamic. Despite their frequent conflicts, Thor and Loki share a bond forged through numerous adventures and mutual respect. However, Loki's deceit and penchant for trouble often strain this relationship. One of the most tragic examples of Loki's treachery is his involvement in the death of Baldr, which would lead to Loki's eventual punishment.

Key myths involving Loki highlight both his helpful and harmful tendencies. One such story is the theft of Idun's apples. Idun, the goddess who guarded the golden apples of immortality, was kidnapped by the giant Thiazi with Loki's reluctant help. However, realizing the gravity of the situation, Loki transformed into a falcon and rescued Idun, restoring the gods' youth and vitality. This tale exemplifies Loki's role as both the cause and solution to the gods' problems.

Another significant myth is the birth of Loki's monstrous offspring: Fenrir, Jormungandr, and Hel. Each of these beings plays an integral role in the cosmology of Norse mythology. Fenrir, the giant wolf, is destined to kill Odin during Ragnarok. Jormungandr, the Midgard Serpent, is fated to battle Thor, resulting in mutual destruction. Hel, the ruler of the underworld, governs the realm where many souls reside after death. These children, born from Loki's union with the giantess Angrboda, symbolize the chaos and destruction that Loki's actions can bring despite his occasional moments of heroism.

Loki's binding and punishment for his betrayal is a significant event in Norse mythology. After causing Baldr's death and engaging in various acts of mischief, Loki is finally captured by the gods. He is bound to a rock with the entrails of his own son, with a venomous serpent placed above him to drip poison onto his face. His wife, Sigyn, stays by his side, catching the venom in a bowl to spare him from the pain. However, when she leaves to empty the bowl, the poison drips onto Loki, causing him to writhe in agony. This punishment serves as a stark reminder of the consequences of Loki's actions, even as it highlights the loyalty and love Sigyn holds for him.

Loki's ability to navigate the thin line between order and chaos makes him a figure of endless fascination. His actions, whether helpful or harmful, drive many of the key events in Norse mythology, shaping the destiny of gods and humans alike. Through his clever solutions, deceitful schemes, and ultimate punishment, Loki embodies the complexities of change and the duality of existence. His stories remind us of the thin line between creation and destruction and the unpredictable nature of life itself.

FREYJA: THE GODDESS OF LOVE, BEAUTY, AND WAR

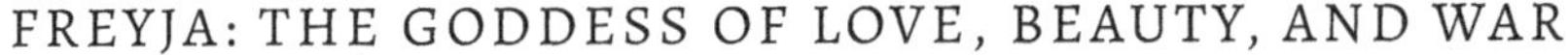

Freyja, one of the most beloved figures in Norse mythology, embodies a blend of love, beauty, and war. She is a goddess of fertility and sensuality, revered for her ability to bring life and abundance. Freyja's domain over love is significant, influencing relationships and desires. Her beauty is unmatched, often described as radiant and enchanting. Beyond just a figure of allure and affection, however, Freyja was also a fierce warrior. As a leader of the Valkyries, the choosers of the slain, Freyja guides fallen warriors to Valhalla, playing a fundamental role in the afterlife and the preparation for Ragnarok.

Freyja's attributes and symbols are rich with meaning and significance. One of her most famous artifacts is the Brisingamen necklace, a dazzling piece that symbolizes her beauty and allure. The story of how she acquired it is a testament to her determination. To obtain Brisingamen, Freyja struck a deal with four dwarves, spending a night with each in exchange for the necklace. This sacrifice highlights her willingness to pursue what she desires, no matter the cost. Another key symbol of Freyja is her chariot, pulled by two large cats. This unique mode of transport underscores her connection to both the domestic and the wild, blending grace with ferocity. Additionally, Freyja possesses a falcon cloak that grants her the power of flight, allowing her to traverse the realms easily. This cloak symbolizes her freedom and her ability to transcend boundaries, both physical and metaphorical.

Freyja's personality is as multifaceted as her domains. She is passionate and determined, never shying away from pursuing her desires. Her quest for beauty and love is relentless, driving many of her actions and decisions. Yet, she is also a devoted and caring figure, deeply connected to those she loves. This duality is evident in her search for her lost husband, Od. When Od disappeared, Freyja embarked on a tireless journey to find him, weeping tears of gold in her sorrow. This story reflects her deep emotional capacity and her unwavering commitment to love.

Freyja's multifaceted nature makes her a captivating and enduring figure in Norse mythology. Through her passionate pursuits, deep emotional connections, and fierce independence, Freyja embodies the vivid spectrum of human experience. As you explore these stories, you will find that Freyja's influence is as significant as it is enduring, a testament to the power of the divine feminine.

Understanding these gods and goddesses will help you see how they shape the very fabric of Norse mythology. Their stories are not just tales of the past but continue to resonate, influencing modern culture and our understanding of the world. As we move forward, we will explore the heroes and legendary figures who further enrich this mythological landscape. These characters, with their epic quests and timeless struggles, offer even more layers to the intricate web of Norse myths.

3

HEROES AND LEGENDARY FIGURES

What makes a hero truly legendary? Is it their strength, cunning, or unyielding courage in the face of insurmountable odds? In Norse mythology, these qualities converge in the figure of Sigurd, a hero whose tale of bravery and wisdom has inspired countless generations. His story is full of adventure, filled with dragons, treasure, and the timeless struggle between good and evil.

SIGURD AND THE DRAGON FAFNIR

Sigurd's legend begins with his remarkable lineage and his mentor, Regin. Born to the noble house of the Völsung, Sigurd was destined for greatness. His father, Sigmund, was a hero in his own right, and his mother, Hjordis, ensured that Sigurd inherited a legacy of valor and nobility. After his parents died, Sigurd was raised by King Hjalprek under the watchful eye of his foster father, Regin. Regin, a master blacksmith and a being of great knowledge, saw in Sigurd the potential to achieve the impossible. He became Sigurd's mentor, guiding him in the ways of combat and strategy. However, Regin harbored a deep-seated desire for vengeance against his brother, Fafnir, who had transformed into a fearsome dragon to guard a vast treasure hoard.

The journey toward slaying Fafnir began with the creation of the sword, Gram. Regin forged this legendary weapon from the fragments of Sigurd's father's shattered sword. Gram was no ordinary blade; it was imbued with the strength to cut through the toughest of scales and the hardest of stones. With Gram in hand, Sigurd set out to confront Fafnir, determined to rid the world of the dragon's malevolence. The encounter with Fafnir was nothing short of epic. Sigurd dug a trench and lay in wait beneath it. As Fafnir slithered to the river to drink, Sigurd thrust Gram upwards, piercing the dragon's heart. The beast's death throes shook the earth, but Sigurd remained steadfast, his courage unwavering.

The significance of the Fafnir myth extends beyond the mere act of slaying a dragon. It explores themes of bravery and heroism, showcasing Sigurd's fearlessness in the face of a seemingly invincible foe. His willingness to confront and defeat Fafnir speaks to the Norse ideal of valor and the importance of facing one's fears head-on. However, the story also explores the darker side of human nature, particularly the consequences of greed. Fafnir's transformation into a dragon was driven by his insatiable desire to hoard treasure, a decision that ultimately led to his demise. The treasure itself, while vast, was cursed, serving as a reminder of the perils of avarice.

Sigurd's wisdom and cunning are highlighted in the aftermath of Fafnir's death. As he cooked the dragon's heart on Regin's request, Sigurd accidentally tasted its blood, which granted him the ability to understand the language of birds. Aware of Regin's treacherous intentions, the birds warned Sigurd of his mentor's plan to kill him and claim the treasure for himself. Armed with this knowledge, Sigurd preemptively struck, killing Regin and securing the treasure for himself. This episode highlights Sigurd's ability to use wit and strategy to navigate the complexities of his quest, showcasing his intelligence and physical prowess.

Sigurd's story is great, inspiring numerous literary works and adaptations and cementing his place as one of the greatest heroes in mythology. The Völsunga saga, a cornerstone of Norse literature, chronicles Sigurd's exploits in detail, highlighting his significance within the cultural narrative. The saga's themes of bravery, wisdom, and the consequences of greed continue to resonate, influencing modern interpretations of heroism and adventure.

THE SAGA OF RAGNAR LOTHBROK

Ragnar Lothbrok, a name that echoes through the ages, is a figure shrouded in both history and myth. Born to the Danish king Sigurd Ring, Ragnar's lineage was one of nobility and strength. His early life was marked by the tales of his father's exploits, planting the seeds of ambition in the young Ragnar. Ragnar's path to greatness began to take shape as he grew. His early exploits included the marriage to the formidable shieldmaiden Lagertha. Their union was one of love, mutual respect, and strength, as Lagertha herself was a warrior of great renown. Ragnar's rise to power was marked by his tactical brilliance and unyielding courage, qualities that would define his legendary status.

Ragnar's adventures are the stuff of legend, with tales that continue to captivate the imagination. One of his most notable exploits was the siege of Paris. In a daring and innovative maneuver, Ragnar and his fleet of longships sailed up the Seine River, breaching the city's defenses in a way that had never been done before. His use of cunning strategies, such as constructing fortifications and employing psychological warfare, showcased his tactical brilliance. This siege demonstrated Ragnar's military prowess and cemented his reputation as a formidable Viking leader. Another remarkable adventure involved Ragnar's encounter with a giant serpent. According to legend, the fearless warrior Ragnar confronted the beast and emerged victorious. This feat added to his growing legend, portraying him as a hero capable of overcoming even the most insurmountable challenges.

The themes of Ragnar's saga are rich with cultural values and lessons that resonate deeply within Norse mythology. At the heart of Ragnar's story is the importance of courage. His willingness to face danger head-on, whether in battle or in the face of mythical creatures, embodies the Norse ideal of bravery. Tactical brilliance is another key theme, with Ragnar's innovative strategies and cunning plans as evidence of intellect's value in warfare. His ability to outsmart and outmaneuver his enemies highlights the importance of wit and strategy in achieving victory. The concept of fate and destiny also plays a significant role in Ragnar's saga. His life, marked by triumph and tragedy, reflects the Norse belief in the inevitability of fate. Despite his many successes, Ragnar's eventual capture and death in a pit of snakes underscore the inescapable nature of destiny.

Ragnar's legacy extends far beyond his lifetime, leaving an indelible mark on Norse and modern culture. His story has inspired countless sagas and historical accounts, with his name appearing in various texts, including Saxo Grammaticus's *Gesta Danorum* and the Icelandic poem "Krákumál." While often romanticized, these accounts have helped preserve Ragnar's legend for future generations. In modern times, Ragnar's tale has found new life in popular culture. The TV series *Vikings* has brought his story to a global audience, portraying Ragnar as a complex and multifaceted character. This portrayal has revived interest in Norse mythology and introduced Ragnar Lothbrok to a new generation of admirers. His influence is seen in various novels, films, and other media, where his exploits and character continue to inspire and captivate.

BRYNHILDR: THE VALKYRIE AND SHIELDMAIDEN

Brynhildr's origins and role in Norse mythology are as captivating as her deeds. She is a Valkyrie, one of Odin's chosen warrior maidens tasked with selecting the bravest of the slain to join the ranks of the Einherjar in Valhalla. Valkyries, in their glittering armor and riding swift, ethereal steeds, soar over battlefields, deciding who will live and who will die. Brynhildr, in particular, is renowned for her beauty, wisdom, and martial prowess. Her divine heritage and her role in the celestial hierarchy underscore her importance.

However, this didn't make her without flaws. After once defying Odin's orders by choosing the wrong warrior in battle to go to Valhalla, she is condemned to a deep slumber, encircled by a wall of fire, awaiting a hero brave enough to rescue her. This image of Brynhildr, clad in divine armor and surrounded by flames, is iconic. It symbolizes her strength, resilience, and the high stakes of her defiance. The ring of fire surrounding her during her enchanted sleep is a symbol of her isolation and the intense trials that define her existence.

Fortunately, during her time of punishment, her fate would intertwine with the hero Sigurd in a tragic love story. According to legend, Sigurd awakens Brynhildr from her enchanted sleep, surrounded by a ring of fire. Moved by her beauty and strength, Sigurd pledges his love to her. However, their love story is marred by manipulation and deceit. Under the influence of a potion, Sigurd forgets Brynhildr and marries another. Heartbroken and enraged, Brynhildr orchestrates Sigurd's death, leading to a tragic end for both lovers. This myth highlights the intensity of their bond and the destructive power of betrayal.

Brynhildr's story holds deep cultural significance, weaving together themes of love, betrayal, and honor. Her romance with Sigurd, one of Norse mythology's most poignant tales, reveals the complexity of love and the painful consequences of broken promises. The involvement of Gudrun, Sigurd's wife, further intensifies the drama, as Brynhildr's love and quest for vengeance set in motion events that intertwine the fates of many. Her unwavering love for Sigurd, despite his betrayal, underscores the intensity of human emotions even divine beings cannot escape, and her decision to seek vengeance speaks to the Norse value of loyalty. Her tragic fate, joining Sigurd in death, highlights the fine line between love and hate and the inevitable consequences of betrayal. Today, Brynhildr's tale continues to resonate, embodying timeless themes that reflect the values and beliefs of the ancient Norse people while offering a poignant window into the complexities of both the human and divine experience.

EGIL SKALLAGRIMSSON: POET AND WARRIOR

Egil Skallagrimsson was born into a family with a formidable legacy. His father, Skallagrim, was a renowned warrior and a figure of immense strength and skill. This lineage shaped Egil's upbringing, embedding in him the qualities of a fierce warrior and a gifted poet. From a young age, Egil displayed remarkable talents. His early poems, composed as a child, hinted at the prodigious skill he would later fully realize. His poetic talent was matched by his prowess in battle, making him a figure of both intellectual and physical might. Egil's family background was a foundation that influenced every aspect of his life, guiding his actions and decisions.

Egil's life was marked by numerous exploits that showcased his dual talents. One of his most famous adventures was his participation in battles and duels, where his combat skills were on full display. His strength and ferocity on the battlefield were unmatched, earning him a fearsome reputation. One notable episode was Egil's journey to England, where he sought to avenge the death of his brother Thorolf. This journey led him to the court of King Æthelstan, where Egil's formidable presence and skills caught the king's attention. The interaction between Egil and Æthelstan highlighted Egil's martial abilities and his diplomatic acumen. He managed to navigate the complexities of the English court, securing favor and rewards from the king.

Egil's talents were not confined to the battlefield. His poetry complemented his warrior prowess, adding depth to his character. Skaldic poetry, known for its complex structure and rich imagery, was Egil's chosen form of expression. His compositions were powerful and evocative, often reflecting the themes of his life and the world around him. One of the most remarkable instances where Egil's poetry played a significant role was when he used it to save his life. Captured by King Eiríkr Bloodaxe, Egil composed the poem "Höfuthlausn" (Head Ransom) overnight, praising the king in a unique meter. This act of poetic brilliance saved his life and showcased the value of wit and intellect. Egil's ability to negotiate peace and influence through his poetry underscored the power of words and the importance of intellectual skill alongside physical strength.

The legacy of Egil Skallagrimsson in Norse culture is enduring and far-reaching. His poems, preserved in the Icelandic sagas, continue to be studied and admired for their artistic and historical significance. The *Egils Saga*, attributed to Snorri Sturluson, is a treasure trove of Egil's adventures, offering insights into his life and the world he inhabited. This saga, rich in detail and narrative complexity, has cemented Egil's place in the pantheon of Norse heroes. His influence extends beyond his lifetime, impacting later Norse literature and culture. The themes and styles of Egil's poetry have inspired subsequent generations of poets and writers, ensuring that his legacy lives on.

Egil's story, with its blend of action and introspection, offers a unique perspective on the Norse ideal of heroism. His early life, shaped by his formidable family, set the stage for a life marked by notable exploits and achievements. His participation in battles, his journey to England, and his interaction with King Æthelstan are just a few examples of his remarkable adventures. The dual talents of poetry and combat that defined Egil's character highlight the Norse appreciation for intellectual and physical prowess. Egil's poems, preserved in the sagas, continue to resonate, reflecting the timeless nature of his legacy and the enduring power of his words.

HARALD FAIRHAIR: THE FIRST KING OF NORWAY

Harald Fairhair's quest for unification began with a bold and ambitious vow: He would not cut his hair until he succeeded in unifying Norway under his rule. This promise was a public declaration of his determination and vision. Harald's commitment earned him the epithet "Fairhair" after he finally cut his hair, which had grown long and unruly during his campaign. This nickname highlighted his dedication and became a symbol of his triumph and the new era he ushered in for Norway.

Several key battles and strategic alliances marked Harald's journey to unify Norway. One of the most significant confrontations was the Battle of Hafrsfjord, which took place around 872 AD. This decisive battle saw Harald clashing with a coalition of regional chieftains who opposed his quest for power. Utilizing superior tactics and a well-organized fleet, Harald emerged victorious. The victory at Hafrsfjord was a turning point, solidifying his control over the western regions of Norway and paving the way for further consolidation. Harald's military campaigns were not solely about brute force; they also involved forming strategic alliances and navigating complex relationships with other chieftains. Some leaders chose to align with Harald, recognizing the benefits of a unified kingdom, while others resisted and faced the might of his forces. Through a combination of diplomacy and warfare, Harald systematically extended his influence across the fragmented territories of Norway.

The themes of leadership and ambition are central to Harald's story, offering valuable cultural lessons. A vision of a unified and stronger Norway drove Harald's quest for power. His leadership style combined decisive action with the ability to inspire loyalty among his followers. The concept of kingship and central authority, as embodied by Harald, marked a significant shift from the fragmented rule of local chieftains to a more centralized and cohesive governance. This transition was not without challenges, as it required balancing ambition with effective leadership. Harald's ability to control a diverse and often contentious group of chieftains demonstrated his strategic acumen and adaptability. His reign exemplified the Norse ideal of a strong, visionary leader who could bring order and stability to a divided land.

Harald Fairhair's legacy is great, with lasting impacts on Norway and Norse culture. His successful unification of Norway laid the foundation for the establishment of a centralized Norwegian kingdom. This achievement strengthened the country's internal cohesion and enhanced its ability to project power externally. Harald's reign is often credited with initiating a period of relative peace and stability, which allowed for economic growth and cultural development. His influence extended beyond his lifetime, as subsequent Norwegian kings built upon his legacy to further consolidate and expand the kingdom. Harald's story has been preserved in various sagas and historical accounts, celebrating his achievements and reinforcing his status as a pivotal figure in Norway's history.

HERVOR: THE WARRIOR MAIDEN AND HER CURSED SWORD

Hervor's story is steeped in the legacy of her father, Angantyr, a formidable berserker who wielded the enchanted sword Tyrfing. This sword was no ordinary weapon; crafted by dwarves, it was unbreakable and possessed incredible power. However, it also carried a deadly curse, bringing misfortune and death to its bearer. Hervor, born into this legacy, was determined to claim her birthright despite the ominous fate tied to Tyrfing. Raised in an environment where tales of valor and supernatural prowess were common, Hervor grew up fiercely determined to retrieve the cursed sword and assert her place within her storied lineage.

Hervor's quest for Tyrfing led her to the haunted island of Samsø, a place shrouded in mystery and fear. The island was said to be inhabited by the restless spirits of the dead, including her father's ghost, which guarded Tyrfing. Hervor's journey was fraught with peril, but her resolve never wavered. As she arrived on the island, she called out to her father's spirit with unwavering courage, demanding that Tyrfing be returned to her. Her confrontation with Angantyr's ghost was a test of her bravery. The spirit, initially resistant, was moved by Hervor's determination and eventually relented, allowing her to take the sword. This moment was a testament to Hervor's unyielding spirit and willingness to face even the most daunting challenges to claim what was rightfully hers.

The significance of Tyrfing lies in its unbreakable power and the curse that brought tragedy to all who wielded it, underscoring the dangers of unchecked power. Hervor's decision to retrieve the cursed sword, fully aware of its deadly history, highlights the themes of bravery, determination, and the burdens of legacy. By accepting Tyrfing and its curse, she embodies the belief in confronting one's fate, no matter the cost. Her journey to claim the sword from her father's spirit is both a physical and metaphorical quest, symbolizing the challenges of inheritance and the responsibilities that come with power.

These stories of heroes and legendary figures showcase individual valor and cunning and also echo the broader themes of Norse mythology. They remind us of the enduring values of courage, legacy, and the human spirit's resilience. As we move forward, we will explore the mythical creatures and beings that populate these rich narratives, further illuminating the intricate web of Norse myths.

4

MYTHICAL CREATURES AND BEINGS

Have you ever imagined a world teeming with mystical creatures, each with its own story, power, and role in the grand cosmos? Norse mythology is a realm where the natural and supernatural coexist, weaving a rich narrative that includes gods, giants, and an array of fantastical beings. These creatures are integral to the myths that shaped the Viking worldview. Among these beings, few are as fearsome and significant as Fenrir, the monstrous wolf whose destiny is intertwined with the fate of the gods.

FENRIR: THE MONSTROUS WOLF AND HIS PROPHECY

Fenrir's origins are as dramatic as his role in Norse mythology. Born to Loki, the trickster god, and the giantess Angrboda, Fenrir is one of three siblings, each destined for significant roles. His brother, Jormungandr, is the Midgard Serpent, and his sister, Hel, rules the realm of the dead. This lineage places Fenrir within a family of formidable and often fearsome beings, each contributing to the balance of power and chaos in the cosmos. The gods, aware of the potential threat posed by Loki's offspring, took measures to control these powerful beings. While Jormungandr was cast into the sea to encircle Midgard and Hel was relegated to the underworld, Fenrir's fate was more complex and closely watched.

Prophecies surrounding Fenrir paint a grim picture. It was foretold that during Ragnarok, the end of the world, Fenrir would break free from his bonds and wreak havoc upon the gods. The gods' first attempts to bind Fenrir were with chains, but these efforts proved futile. The first chain, Leyding, was crafted with great effort, yet Fenrir easily shattered it. The gods then forged a second, stronger chain named Dromi, believing it would hold the mighty wolf. However, Fenrir also broke free from Dromi, his strength proving greater than the gods had anticipated. These failures only heightened their fear and desperation. Realizing they needed something far beyond ordinary means, the gods turned to the dwarves, master craftsmen known for their unparalleled skill and magical prowess.

The dwarves of Svartalfheim accepted the challenge and forged Gleipnir, a magical ribbon unlike any other. Gleipnir was made from six impossibilities: the sound of a cat's footsteps, the beard of a woman, the roots of a mountain, the sinews of a bear, the breath of a fish, and the spittle of a bird. Despite its delicate appearance, Gleipnir was as strong as it was thin, capable of binding even the most powerful of beings. Now armed with this extraordinary ribbon, the gods approached Fenrir with a new plan.

To persuade Fenrir to allow himself to be bound by Gleipnir, the gods proposed it as a test of strength. Fenrir, suspicious of their intentions, agreed only if one of the gods would place their hand in his mouth as a pledge of good faith. Tyr, the god of war and courage, volunteered, knowing the risk involved. As the gods bound Fenrir with Gleipnir, the wolf struggled but could not break free. Realizing he had been deceived, Fenrir clamped down on Tyr's hand, severing it. Tyr's sacrifice was immense, symbolizing his unwavering commitment to the gods and his courage in the face of inevitable loss.

With Fenrir successfully bound, the gods took further measures to ensure he could not escape. They secured him to a boulder and placed a sword between his jaws to keep them open, preventing him from biting anyone else. Fenrir's reaction was one of rage and helplessness, his mighty roars echoing through the realms. This binding of Fenrir was an act of control over chaos and destiny. It represented the gods' ability to impose order on the primal forces threatening their world.

The symbolic meaning of Fenrir's binding is multifaceted. It highlights the delicate balance between freedom and restraint, illustrating how even the most powerful beings can be subdued through cunning and cooperation. Tyr's sacrifice is a testament to courage and duty, emphasizing the personal costs of protecting the greater good. The story of Fenrir's binding also underscores the themes of control and destiny in Norse mythology. The gods' efforts to contain Fenrir reflect their ongoing struggle to maintain order against the ever-present forces of chaos.

JORMUNGANDR: THE MIDGARD SERPENT

From the moment of Jormungandr's birth, also known as the Midgard Serpent, it was clear that he was destined for greatness and fear. Recognizing the creature's potential danger, Odin casts him into the sea that encircles Midgard, the world of humans. There, the serpent grew to an immense size, eventually reaching the point where he could encircle the entire world and grasp his own tail. This image of Jormungandr encircling Midgard is iconic, signifying the boundaries of the world and the relentless nature of time.

One key myth involving Jormungandr is when Thor goes on a fishing expedition with Hymir, the giant, a tale that captures the tension and animosity between the two. In this story, Thor and Hymir set out to catch Jormungandr using an ox head as bait. As Thor manages to hook the mighty serpent, an ensuing struggle takes place between Thor and Jormungandr, churning the sea violently. Just as Thor is about to deliver a fatal blow with his hammer, Mjölnir, Hymir, terrified by the sight, cuts the line, allowing Jormungandr to escape, leading to what would become a grave mistake.

Reunited in rivalry, the two would meet again during Ragnarok, the world's end. According to prophecy, Jormungandr and Thor are destined to kill each other in this cataclysmic event. As the end of the world approaches, Jormungandr rises from the sea, joining the forces of chaos against the gods. Thor ultimately slays Jormungandr with his hammer, but not before the serpent releases a deadly venom that fatally wounds Thor. The mutual destruction of Thor and Jormungandr marks a pivotal moment in Ragnarok, underscoring the themes of destruction and renewal that permeate Norse mythology.

THE VALKYRIES: CHOOSERS OF THE SLAIN

Valkyries are iconic female figures revered for their roles and feared for their power. These warrior maidens serve Odin, the Allfather, in selecting which warriors will be taken to Valhalla, the hall of the slain. Valhalla is not just a resting place for the dead; it is a training ground where chosen warriors, known as the Einherjar, prepare for the final battle of Ragnarok.

The common depiction of Valkyries is both awe-inspiring and formidable. Clad in gleaming armor, these maidens ride winged horses across the skies, descending upon battlefields to fulfill their sacred duty. Wielding spears and shields, they embody the martial prowess and courage they seek in their chosen warriors. Often portrayed with an ethereal beauty that belies their deadly capabilities, they also symbolize the perfect blend of grace and strength, harbingers of death and glory, as they guide the souls of fallen heroes to their eternal reward.

One of the most famous myths involving Valkyries is the story of Brynhildr, a Valkyrie who defied Odin's wishes, choosing the unfavorable outcome of a battle. As punishment, Odin cast her into a deep sleep, surrounded by a ring of fire, until a hero brave enough to pass through the flames would awaken her. As we discussed before, Sigurd, the legendary hero, succeeded in this task, leading to a tragic love story that intertwined their fates. Brynhildr's defiance and the consequences she faced highlight the complex nature of Valkyries, who, despite their immense power, are still bound by the will of the gods.

The Valkyrie's selection process reflects the values of courage, strength, and loyalty central to Norse culture. As selectors, it is their role to uphold these ideals, ensuring that only the worthiest are granted the honor of fighting alongside the gods, serving as a bridge between the mortal and divine realms, and guiding the souls of fallen warriors to their final destination.

DWARVES: MASTER SMITHS AND CREATORS OF MAGICAL ARTIFACTS

Dwarves in Norse mythology are fascinating beings renowned for their unparalleled craftsmanship and deep knowledge of the earth. Their origins are as intriguing as their creations. According to the myths, dwarves were formed from the blood of Ymir, the primordial giant whose body was used to create the world. Emerging from the earth itself, dwarves possess an intrinsic connection to the underground realms, where they ply their trade as master smiths. Their attributes include incredible skill in metalworking and a keen understanding of the magical properties of the natural world. This combination of craftsmanship and mystical knowledge makes them indispensable figures in many Norse myths.

The role of dwarves in Norse mythology extends far beyond mere artisans. They are the creators of some of the most significant and powerful artifacts, each with unique properties and importance. Thor's hammer, Mjölnir, is perhaps the most iconic of these creations. Forged by the dwarven brothers Sindri and Brokkr, Mjölnir symbolizes immense power and protection, capable of leveling mountains and summoning thunder. Odin's spear, Gungnir, crafted by the sons of Ivaldi, is another example. Never missing its target, this spear symbolizes authority, wisdom, and fate. Draupnir, a gold ring replicating itself, is a marvel of abundance and wealth. These artifacts are imbued with the essence of the dwarves' skill and the earth's magic.

At the heart of dwarven lore are the stories celebrating their extraordinary craftsmanship, particularly illustrated in the legends of their most renowned creations. Among these, the tale of Mjölnir's forging is a standout, showcasing their ingenuity and resilience in the face of adversity. This story begins with Loki, the god known for his penchant for mischief, engaging in a wager that leads him to challenge the dwarven brothers Sindri and Brokkr. Loki dares them to create items that would surpass the craftsmanship of the items made by the sons of Ivaldi, another set of skilled dwarf craftsmen who had produced treasures for the gods. Accepting the challenge, Sindri and Brokkr set to work.

Despite Loki's cunning attempts to sabotage their forge work—transforming into a biting fly to distract and harm the brothers at important moments—they succeed in crafting Mjölnir and also Gullinbursti, a boar with bristles of gold that glows in the darkest of nights, and Draupnir, an arm ring that magically produces eight copies of itself every ninth night. The making of Mjölnir, however, did not go unimpeded. Due to Loki's interference, the hammer's handle was fashioned shorter than intended. Despite this, Mjölnir became known as the mightiest weapon in the Norse cosmos, symbolizing protection and the defeat of chaos. This narrative underlines the dwarves' exceptional skills, capable of producing marvels that even the gods covet and rely upon.

Equally as significant of dwarven legends is the crafting of Brisingamen, the magnificent necklace of Freyja, the goddess of love, beauty, and fertility. As previously mentioned, this masterpiece was brought into existence by four dwarven craftsmen whose work was so exquisite that Freyja agreed to a unique form of payment: She would spend one night with each craftsman as compensation for their unparalleled artistry. The creation of Brisingamen highlights the dwarves' exceptional craftsmanship and their astuteness in negotiations that reach into the divine realm. Worn by Freyja, the necklace symbolizes her divine beauty and power and is a testament to the dwarves' status as unrivaled artisans capable of weaving magic and allure into their creations.

In many ways, dwarves represent the Norse appreciation for skill, knowledge, and the unseen forces that shape the world. Their stories, filled with creativity and magic, offer a glimpse into the values and beliefs of the Norse people. The artifacts they create, from Mjölnir to Brisingamen, are objects of power and symbols of the dwarves' enduring legacy in the mythological landscape.

ELVES: THE LIGHT AND DARK ELVES OF ALFHEIM

Elves in Norse mythology are enchanting beings who inhabit the realms of Alfheim. They are divided into two distinct types: the light elves (Ljósálfar) and the dark elves (Dökkálfar). The light elves reside in the ethereal and luminous realm of Alfheim, a place filled with beauty and magic. These beings are often depicted as benevolent and radiant, embodying grace and wisdom. Their appearances are striking, with features that reflect their divine nature. They are closely associated with the forces of light and life, playing roles in promoting growth and harmony.

In contrast, the dark elves are more mysterious and elusive. Often linked to the underground, they are enigmatic and potentially malevolent. Their realm is shrouded in shadows, and their intentions are unclear. While they possess great knowledge and magical abilities, their actions can be unpredictable, adding an element of intrigue and caution to their portrayal.

The roles and attributes of elves are as varied as their appearances. Light elves are known for their benevolence and beauty, often acting as guardians of nature and fertility. They are seen as protectors of the natural world, ensuring the balance and health of the environment. Their presence brings prosperity and joy, and they are frequently invoked in rituals and prayers for good harvests and bountiful seasons. Dark elves, on the other hand, are more enigmatic. Their knowledge of the earth and its hidden secrets makes them powerful beings, but their motives are not always transparent. They are often involved in magical and mystical events, using their abilities to influence outcomes in ways that can be both beneficial and detrimental. This duality adds depth to their character, making them complex figures in the mythological landscape.

One key myth involving elves is their interaction with the god Freyr, who rules over Alfheim. Freyr, a god of fertility and prosperity, has a close relationship with the light elves. This bond is evident in various tales where the elves assist Freyr in his endeavors by enhancing his powers and supporting his efforts to bring abundance to the land. Their cooperation symbolizes the harmony between divine forces and nature, reflecting the interconnectedness of all things. Other myths feature elves in magical events where they aid in the creation of powerful artifacts or intervene in human affairs.

The cultural significance of elves extends beyond their mythological roles. They are deeply woven into Norse beliefs and traditions, symbolizing the connection to nature and fertility. Elves are often associated with the cycles of life, death, and rebirth, reflecting the understanding of the natural world. The belief in elves and their influence persisted through the ages, leaving a lasting impact on later folklore and popular culture. Stories of elves continued to be told, adapting to new contexts and blending with local traditions. This enduring legacy highlights their timeless appeal and the universal themes they represent.

GIANTS (JOTUNN): THE ETERNAL FOES OF THE GODS

Giants, or Jotunn, are among the most ancient beings in Norse mythology, tracing their lineage back to Ymir, the primordial giant. Ymir's immense size and strength were passed down to his descendants, making giants formidable figures in the mythological landscape. These beings are characterized by their colossal stature and extraordinary power, often depicted as towering over both gods and humans. Their origins are steeped in the primordial chaos that existed before the world's creation, embodying nature's raw, untamed forces. The laws of the gods do not bind giants; instead, they exist as a constant challenge to the divine order, representing the universe's untamed and often destructive aspects.

In Norse myths, giants frequently conflict with the gods, particularly the Aesir and Vanir. These battles are physical confrontations that symbolize the ongoing struggle between order and chaos. With their immense strength and primal nature, the giants often oppose the gods' efforts to maintain balance and harmony in the cosmos. However, the relationship between giants and gods is complex and multifaceted. While they are often adversaries, there are instances where giants and gods form alliances or even familial bonds. For example, Loki, although a god, is of giant lineage and frequently interacts with both worlds, often blurring the lines between friend and foe.

One of the most famous myths involving giants is the story of Thrym and the theft of Thor's hammer, Mjölnir. Thrym, a giant king, steals Mjölnir and demands Freyja's hand in marriage as ransom. In a clever twist, Thor disguises himself as Freyja and, with Loki's help, infiltrates Thrym's hall. During the wedding feast, Thor reveals his true identity and reclaims his hammer, using it to defeat Thrym and his kin.

Another significant myth is the building of Asgard's walls by a giant. In this tale, a giant disguised as a mason offers to build an impenetrable wall around Asgard in exchange for the sun, the moon, and Freyja's hand in marriage. The gods, believing the task impossible, agree to the terms. However, with the help of his mighty stallion, the giant makes rapid progress. Fearing the loss of such precious treasures, the gods enlist Loki to sabotage the construction. In doing so, Loki transforms into a mare and lures the stallion away, preventing the giant from completing the wall on time. When the giant's true identity is revealed, Thor swiftly deals with him, ensuring the safety of Asgard. This myth underscores the cunning and resourcefulness of the gods in dealing with the giants' threats.

As we conclude our exploration of mythical creatures and beings, it becomes evident that these characters embody the values, fears, and hopes of the Norse people. From Fenrir's chaotic power to the elves' enigmatic nature, each being plays a role in the rich world of Norse mythology. In the next chapter, we will look at the myths and legends that these creatures inhabit, exploring how their tales reflect the intricate beliefs and cultural heritage of the ancient Norse.

MAKE A DIFFERENCE WITH YOUR REVIEW

"To give without expecting anything in return is true greatness."

People who share stories and knowledge with others live richer lives. So, let's make a difference together!

Would you help someone just like you—curious about Norse mythology but unsure where to begin?

My goal is to make Mythology easy and fun for everyone to learn and experience.

But to share these ancient tales with more readers, I need your help.

Most people decide what to read based on reviews. So, I'm asking you to help a fellow mythology lover by leaving a review.

It costs nothing and takes less than a minute but could spark someone's journey into the world of Norse gods and legends. Your review could help…

- …one more reader discover the powerful stories of Odin, Thor, and Loki.
- …one more fan experience the adventure of mythical heroes and creatures.
- …one more story lover feel the magic of runes and the battles between gods and giants.
- …one more legend come alive.

To make a difference, simply scan the QR code below and leave a review:

If you enjoy sharing the gift of stories, you're my kind of person. Thank you from the bottom of my heart!

- Anthony Poe

5

MYTHS AND LEGENDS

Have you ever contemplated the end of the world as envisioned by ancient cultures? In Norse mythology, this cataclysmic event is known as Ragnarok or the Twilight of the Gods. It is not just an end but a dramatic series of events that dismantle the existing world order, only to pave the way for a new beginning. The prophecy of Ragnarok is a cornerstone of Norse beliefs, rich with symbolism and meaning that continues to intrigue and inspire.

RAGNAROK: THE TWILIGHT OF THE GODS

The prophecy of Ragnarok foretells a series of events that will culminate in the destruction of the cosmos and the death gods. The signs leading up to Ragnarok are as ominous as they are inevitable. One of the most significant harbingers is Fimbulwinter, a relentless, three-year-long winter that plunges the world into darkness and despair. This brutal winter is marked by bitter cold, ceaseless snow, and a breakdown of social order as people turn against one another in their struggle to survive. Alongside

Fimbulwinter, other portents include the breaking of bonds that have long held the forces of chaos at bay. Fenrir, the monstrous wolf, will break free from his magical restraints, and Jormungandr, the Midgard Serpent, will rise from the ocean and cause massive tidal waves and flooding.

Key figures play pivotal roles in the unfolding of Ragnarok. Odin, the Allfather, prepares for the ultimate battle, knowing his fate is sealed. Thor, the god of thunder, readies himself to face Jormungandr, while Loki, now fully embracing his role as an agent of chaos, leads an army of giants and other monstrous beings against the gods. Fenrir, whose strength and fury have grown unbounded, is destined to confront Odin in a deadly encounter. Heimdall, the watchman of the gods, sounds the Gjallarhorn, a mighty horn that echoes through the heavens, signaling the commencement of the final battle.

The events of Ragnarok are a mix of epic battles and tragic outcomes. As the gods and giants clash, the cosmos trembles. Odin faces Fenrir, and despite his formidable prowess, he is ultimately devoured by the monstrous wolf. In a poignant act of vengeance, Odin's son Vidar slays Fenrir, avenging his father's death. Thor and Jormungandr engage in a titanic struggle, and though Thor manages to kill the serpent, he succumbs to its deadly venom shortly after. Loki and Heimdall, eternally locked in opposition, meet their end at each other's hands. The sun and moon are swallowed by wolves, plunging the world into darkness. The earth itself shakes and splits, consumed by fire and water, and sinks into the sea.

The themes of fate and renewal are deeply woven into the fabric of Ragnarok. The Norse cosmos operates on a cyclical understanding of time, where destruction is not an end but a necessary precursor to renewal. The inevitability of fate is a central tenet, as even the gods cannot escape their destined roles. Yet, a new one emerges from the ashes of the old world. The earth rises again, fresh and verdant, free from the scars of the past. Baldr, the beloved god slain by Loki's treachery, returns from the underworld, symbolizing hope and the continuity of life. Two human survivors, Lif and Lifthrasir, emerge from Yggdrasil, the World Tree, to repopulate the earth, ensuring the cycle of life continues.

Ragnarok holds cultural significance, encapsulating the eternal struggle between order and chaos, a theme that resonates deeply within the Norse worldview. The gods' valiant stand against overwhelming odds exemplifies the Norse ideal of bravery and honor in the face of certain doom. Moreover, the concept of renewal and rebirth after destruction offers a sense of hope and continuity. It reflects the Norse understanding that life, despite its inevitable hardships and ultimate end, is part of a greater, unending cycle. This belief in the cyclical nature of existence permeates Norse mythology, reinforcing the interconnectedness of life, death, and rebirth.

In essence, Ragnarok is a deep allegory for the resilience of life and the perpetual dance between creation and destruction. It reminds us that even in the darkest of times, there is always the promise of a new dawn, a fresh beginning that carries the legacy of the past into the future.

THE THEFT OF IDUN'S APPLES

Idun, the goddess associated with youth and rejuvenation, holds a special place among the Norse gods. She is the keeper of the golden apples that grant the gods their eternal youth. Without these magical apples, even gods would age and wither. Idun's guardianship of these apples is necessary for maintaining the vitality and strength of the divine beings. Beyond keeping the apples safe, her role is about ensuring the gods remain in their prime, ready to face any challenges that come their way. The golden apples, imbued with powerful magic, symbolize perpetual renewal and the delicate balance of life in Asgard.

The story of the theft of Idun's apples is a tale of cunning and betrayal, primarily involving Loki. It all began when Loki was captured by the giant Thiazi, who demanded a ransom for his release. Thiazi coerced Loki into luring Idun out of Asgard, knowing the invaluable worth of her golden apples. Compelled by the giant's threat, Loki devised a plan. He convinced Idun to step outside the safety of Asgard by promising her even more beautiful apples in a nearby grove. Once outside, Thiazi, in the form of a giant eagle, swooped down and abducted Idun. To prevent her from escaping, Thiazi transformed Idun into a nut and carried her off to his distant mountain lair.

The absence of Idun and her apples quickly took its toll on the gods. They began to age and weaken, their once-vibrant forms now showing signs of decay. Realizing the gravity of the situation, the gods demanded that Loki rectify his wrongdoing. Faced with the wrath of the aging gods, Loki agreed to rescue Idun. He borrowed Freyja's falcon cloak, a magical garment that allowed its wearer to fly. Transforming into a falcon, Loki soared through the skies to Thiazi's mountain fortress. There, he found Idun still in the form of a nut. Carefully, he grasped her in his talons and began the perilous flight back to Asgard.

Upon discovering Idun's absence, Thiazi transformed back into an eagle and gave chase. The pursuit was intense, with Thiazi closing in on Loki as they neared Asgard. Seeing Loki's approach, the gods quickly built a large fire at the gates of Asgard. As Loki and Idun safely crossed the threshold, the gods ignited the flames. Thiazi, unable to stop in time, flew into the fire and was consumed by the flames, meeting his end. With Idun safely back in Asgard, she restored the gods' youth with her golden apples, bringing vigor and vitality back to the divine realm.

The tale of Idun's theft and subsequent rescue carries deep moral and cultural lessons. It highlights the importance of loyalty and the devastating consequences of betrayal. Loki's initial act of deceit nearly brought ruin to the gods, demonstrating how a single act of treachery can have far-reaching effects. Yet, his role in the rescue also shows the possibility of redemption and the restoration of balance. Even divine beings are not immune to the ravages of time, and they are rejuvenated through the magic of the golden apples. This cycle of aging and renewal reflects the natural world, where death and rebirth are part of the eternal cycle of life.

The story also emphasizes the value of resilience and unity among the gods. Despite the challenges and the looming threat of Thiazi, the gods worked together to protect their realm and restore their strength. This unity is evidence of their shared commitment to maintaining the balance and harmony of Asgard. The theft of Idun's apples, with its themes of trust, betrayal, and renewal, offers a rich narrative that continues to resonate, reminding us of the enduring power of youth, the consequences of our actions, and the possibility of redemption.

THOR'S JOURNEY TO JOTUNHEIM

Thor, the thunder god, often ventured into the realm of the giants, Jotunheim, accompanied by an eclectic group of companions. On one notable expedition, Thor was joined by Loki, his ever-unpredictable companion, and the mortal siblings Thialfi and Roskva. Thialfi, known for his extraordinary speed, and Roskva, with her steadfast loyalty, were as much a part of this adventure as the gods themselves. Their journey was fraught with challenges, each testing their resolve and strength.

As they traveled toward Jotunheim, they encountered the formidable river Vimur. The river was swollen and treacherous, its currents threatening to sweep them away. Thor, undeterred, waded into the river, using his immense strength to forge a path. However, the river rose higher, and it seemed as though the very elements conspired against them. Loki, Thialfi, and Roskva struggled to keep pace, the cold waters sapping their energy. Thor, realizing the source of the river's fury, hurled a massive boulder upstream, disrupting the flow and allowing them to cross safely. Though born of brute strength, this act highlighted Thor's ability to adapt and overcome natural obstacles.

Upon reaching the hall of Utgard-Loki, the ruler of the giants, the group was met with various challenges that were as cunning as they were deceptive. Utgard-Loki, aware of Thor's reputation, sought to humble the thunder god through a series of seemingly impossible tasks. Thor's first challenge was to lift a giant cat. Despite his legendary strength, Thor could barely lift one of the cat's paws. It was only later revealed that the cat was, in fact, the Midgard Serpent in disguise, an illusion crafted to confound even the mightiest of gods.

Next, Thor was given a drinking horn and told to drain it in one go. Thor drank deeply, but the horn's contents never seemed to diminish. He drank three mighty gulps, yet the level of the liquid barely lowered. The truth, revealed later, was that the horn was connected to the sea, making it an endless source. Thor's efforts, though Herculean, were no match for the cunning of Utgard-Loki, whose illusions were designed to mock the gods' greatest strengths.

These tests, while humiliating, taught Thor invaluable lessons about the limits of physical strength and the importance of cunning. Thor, known for his brute force, realized that not all battles could be won with sheer power. With their clever illusions, the giants showcased the significance of intellect and strategy.

Culturally, this myth reflects the values of bravery and perseverance. Despite the seemingly insurmountable challenges, Thor's unwavering determination embodies the Norse ideal of facing adversity head-on. Yet, the balance between pride and humility is also a crucial theme. Thor's journey to Jotunheim reminds us that even the mightiest can be brought low by cleverness and guile. This balance is a recurring motif in Norse mythology, reflecting the belief that strength must be tempered with wisdom and humility.

THE DEATH AND RESURRECTION OF BALDR

Baldr, known for his radiant beauty and wisdom, was beloved by all in Asgard. His presence brought light and joy, making his eventual demise all the more tragic. The events leading up to Baldr's death began with a series of ominous dreams. Baldr was haunted by visions of his own death—dreams so vivid and foreboding that they left him deeply troubled. His mother, Frigg, alarmed by these premonitions, took drastic measures to protect him. She traveled across the realms, securing oaths from every living and non-living thing to not harm her son. Stones, metals, animals, and even diseases swore to spare Baldr, making him seemingly invincible.

However, in her exhaustive efforts, Frigg overlooked the humble mistletoe, deeming it too insignificant to pose any threat.

Loki, ever the trickster and driven by his insatiable need for chaos, discovered this oversight. He crafted a slender dart from mistletoe and hatched a plan to use it against Baldr. During a gathering where the gods, amused by Baldr's newfound invulnerability, took turns hurling objects at him, Loki approached Baldr's blind brother, Hodr. Feigning helpfulness, Loki guided Hodr's hand, instructing him to throw the mistletoe dart. The dart struck Baldr, piercing his heart and killing him instantly. The shock and grief that followed were immeasurable. The gods, who had been laughing and jesting moments before, were plunged into deep sorrow. Baldr, the shining god, lay dead, a victim of Loki's treachery.

The gods' mourning for Baldr was deep and heartfelt. Desperate to bring him back, they sent Hermod, another of Odin's sons, to the underworld. Riding the swift and mystical horse Sleipnir, Hermod descended into the depths of Helheim to plead for Baldr's return. Hel, the ruler of the underworld and Loki's daughter, listened to Hermod's plea. She agreed to release Baldr on one condition: Every living and inanimate thing in the cosmos must weep for him. The gods, hopeful and determined, spread the word across the realms. Indeed, everything wept for Baldr—except one being. A giantess named Thokk, widely believed to be Loki in disguise, refused to shed a tear. Her refusal sealed Baldr's fate, and he remained unreachable and lost to the gods in the underworld.

Baldr's death was a pivotal event with far-reaching consequences. According to prophecy, after Ragnarok, the world would be renewed, and Baldr would return from the underworld. His resurrection would symbolize the dawn of a new era, a world reborn from the ashes of the old. Baldr's return would bring hope and renewal, his presence a beacon of light in the new pantheon of gods. This promise of resurrection imbued the myth with a sense of continuity and the enduring nature of life. Baldr's role in the new world underscored the cyclical nature of existence, where there is the promise of rebirth and renewal, even in death.

The tale of Baldr intricately weaves together themes of love, loss, and hope. The gods' deep grief and fervent efforts to reclaim him showcase their deep love and the stark pain of loss. Baldr's demise poignantly underscores the fragility of life, extending even to the divine. However, his prophesied return post-Ragnarok symbolizes hope and life's cyclical nature, echoing the Norse belief in continuous cycles of destruction and rebirth. Baldr's story, rich in emotion and significance, captivates with its exploration of enduring love, the inevitability of loss, and the promise of renewal, embodying timeless themes that continue to inspire.

THE QUEST FOR THE MEAD OF POETRY

In Norse mythology, the Mead of Poetry holds a special place. Its origins are as intriguing as its effects. The mead was created from the blood of Kvasir, the wisest being formed from the spittle of the gods after the Aesir-Vanir War. Kvasir's wisdom was unparalleled, and his blood, mixed with honey by the dwarves Fjalar and Galar, transformed into a mead that granted wisdom and poetic inspiration to anyone who drank it. This mead, known as Óðrœrir, became a coveted source of knowledge and artistic talent.

Odin, the Allfather, embarked on a daring quest to obtain this precious mead. A series of cunning deceptions marked Odin's pursuit. He learned that the giant Suttung had acquired the mead and hidden it in a mountain guarded by his daughter Gunnlod. To gain access, Odin disguised himself and offered his services to Suttung's brother Baugi, performing various tasks to earn his trust. After completing his work, Odin requested a sip of the mead as his reward. Baugi, unable to grant this wish directly, drilled a hole into the mountain where the mead was kept. Transforming into a snake, Odin slithered through the hole, infiltrating Suttung's stronghold.

Once inside, Odin encountered Gunnlod and spent three nights with her, charming her into granting him three sips of the mead. However, Odin's sips were no ordinary draughts; with each sip, he consumed vast quantities of the mead and eventually drank it all. Having secured the mead, Odin transformed into an eagle and fled the mountain. Suttung, upon discovering the theft, also transformed into an eagle and pursued Odin. The chase was fierce, but Odin, with his cunning and the power of the mead, managed to outfly Suttung and reach Asgard. There, he regurgitated the mead into containers, ensuring its safe distribution among the gods and select mortals.

The outcome of Odin's quest for the Mead of Poetry was impactful. By securing the mead, Odin bestowed the gifts of wisdom and poetic inspiration upon humanity. True poets and scholars were said to be those to whom Odin personally dispensed the mead, while the dregs that fell to Midgard inspired less talented individuals. This tale underscores the divine origin of artistic and intellectual talents, emphasizing their value and the lengths one must go to obtain such gifts.

The themes of wisdom and cunning are central to the story of the Mead of Poetry. Odin's quest illustrates the immense value placed on knowledge and the lengths he was willing to go to obtain it. His use of trickery and transformation highlights the importance of cunning and strategy in achieving one's goals. In Norse mythology, obtaining wisdom demands sacrifice, risk, and the ability to outwit formidable foes. Odin's relentless pursuit of the mead reflects his insatiable thirst for knowledge and his role as a seeker of wisdom.

In this chapter, we have explored the rich tapestry of Norse myths and legends, each tale offering unique insights into the values and beliefs of the ancient Norse people. From the cataclysmic events of Ragnarok to the enchanting quest for the Mead of Poetry, these stories continue to captivate and inspire. In the next chapter, we will explore the rituals, symbols, and practices that shaped Norse culture, further illuminating the intricate world of Norse mythology.

6

RITUALS, SYMBOLS, AND PRACTICES

Imagine standing in the heart of a Viking settlement, surrounded by your kin, as the chieftain raises his voice in a powerful invocation to the gods. The air is thick with anticipation and the scent of burning wood. This is Blót, one of the most significant rituals in Norse paganism, where offerings are made to honor the gods and seek their favor. Blót was not just a simple act of sacrifice but an expression of reciprocity between humans and the divine. It was a way to maintain balance and ensure the community's well-being.

BLÓT: SACRIFICIAL RITUALS AND OFFERINGS

The primary purpose of Blót was to gain favor from the gods, spirits, and ancestors. These rituals were performed to ensure good harvests, successful hunts, and protection from harm. The offerings made during Blót were seen as gifts to the gods, who, in turn, would bestow blessings upon the people. This exchange was rooted in the belief that the relationship between humans and deities was mutual, give and take. Animals were the most common offerings, with livestock like pigs, goats, and cattle sacrificed to appease the gods. Food and drink were also offered in some cases, symbolizing the sustenance provided by the earth and the gods themselves. There are even accounts of human sacrifices during particularly dire times, though these were rare and reserved for the most critical circumstances.

Conducting a Blót involved carefully orchestrated steps, each imbued with symbolic meaning. The preparation began with choosing a suitable sacrificial site, often a sacred grove or a specially designated area within the community. Participants gathered, bringing their offerings and wearing their finest clothes as a sign of respect. The chieftain or a designated gothi (priest) led the ceremony, starting with prayers and invocations to the gods, calling upon their presence and favor. The act of sacrifice followed, where the chosen animal was ritually slain and its blood collected in a ceremonial bowl. This blood was considered sacred and was sprinkled on the participants, the altar, and the statues of the gods as a means of sanctification. The meat from the sacrifice was then prepared and shared among the community in a communal feast, symbolizing unity and the shared blessings of the gods.

Blót was performed on various occasions, each with its own significance. Seasonal Blót, such as those held during Yule and Midsummer, marked important points in the agricultural calendar, ensuring fertility and prosperity. These celebrations were grand events involving the entire community and often lasted several days. Personal Blót, on the other hand, was conducted for specific milestones like weddings, births, and even funerals. These rituals provided an opportunity to seek divine favor and blessings for significant life events, reinforcing the bond between the individual and the divine.

The communal aspect of Blót is also important to note. Beyond appeasing the gods, these rituals were about reinforcing social bonds within the community. The chieftain or gothi played an important role as a religious leader and a unifying figure who embodied the community's collective aspirations and fears. The communal feast that followed the sacrificial act was a time for fellowship, storytelling, and celebration. It allowed the people to come together, share their fortunes, and strengthen their sense of belonging. This social cohesion was vital for the survival and prosperity of the community, especially in the harsh and unpredictable environment of the Viking Age.

Blót was a cornerstone of Norse religious practice, a powerful expression of the interconnectedness between humans, gods, and the natural world. It was a time of reverence, reflection, and renewal, where the boundaries between the mortal and the divine blurred, and the community reaffirmed its place in the grand cosmic order. As you dive deeper into these rituals, you will discover the beliefs and values that shaped the lives of the Norse people, offering timeless lessons that continue to resonate today.

SEIDR: THE MAGIC OF PROPHECY AND SHAMANISM

Imagine a world where the boundaries between the seen and unseen are fluid, where one can tap into the mystical forces that shape fate and reality. This is the realm of Seidr, an ancient form of Norse magic that held a significant place in Viking culture. Seidr was a practice that transcended the ordinary, involving prophecy, healing, and even curse-casting. Both gods and humans practiced Seidr, making it a bridge between the divine and the mortal. It was a powerful tool that allowed practitioners to influence events, communicate with spirits, and gain insight into the unknown.

Seidr rituals were elaborate and required specific techniques to enter trance states. Practitioners often used chanting, drumming, and rhythmic movements to induce these altered states of consciousness. The rhythmic beats of drums and the melodic chants created a hypnotic atmosphere, transporting the Seidr practitioner into a trance where they could access hidden realms. Ritual objects like staves and wands were central to these ceremonies. These items were extensions of the practitioner's will and intent, amplifying their connection to the spiritual world. The staff, often made from sacred wood, symbolized the practitioner's authority and power to navigate the mystical realms.

The practitioners of Seidr held a unique position in Norse society. Female practitioners, known as Volva or seeresses, were highly respected and often sought after for their wisdom and guidance. The Volva played an essential role in the community, offering protection, healing, and acting as mediators in disputes. They were revered for their ability to communicate with spirits and foresee future events, making them indispensable in daily life and during times of crisis. Male practitioners, called Seidrmen, faced a more complex social standing. While their abilities were acknowledged, practicing Seidr was often seen as unmanly, risking their honor and social status. Despite this, some men, including the god Odin, embraced Seidr for the knowledge it offered.

Key myths involving Seidr highlight its significance and the complex attitudes toward it. One notable story is how Freyja, the goddess of love and war, taught Seidr to the Aesir gods. Freyja was considered the foremost practitioner of Seidr, and her knowledge of this magic was unparalleled. She introduced the Aesir to the practice, emphasizing its importance in understanding and manipulating fate. Freyja's role in spreading Seidr underscores her multifaceted nature and influence over the divine and mortal realms.

Odin's use of Seidr is another compelling example. The Allfather's quest for wisdom led him to embrace Seidr despite its social stigma. Odin's determination to gain knowledge of the future and control over fate drove him to undergo rigorous rituals and sacrifices. His use of Seidr was part of his broader pursuit of understanding the cosmos and mastering its secrets. This aspect of Odin's character highlights the lengths he would go to acquire wisdom, even if it meant defying societal norms.

The practice of Seidr was not without its complexities. While it offered immense power and insight, it also carried risks and moral ambiguities. Practitioners could use Seidr for beneficial and harmful purposes, leading to mixed social attitudes toward them. Some viewed Seidr as a noble pursuit of knowledge and healing, while others saw it as a dangerous and potentially malevolent force. This duality reflects the broader themes in Norse mythology, where the lines between good and evil, order and chaos, are often blurred.

Seidr's legacy extends beyond ancient times, finding a resurgence in modern neo-pagan and Ásatrú communities. Contemporary practitioners seek to rediscover and adapt traditional Seidr techniques, emphasizing personal growth, self-discovery, and a deeper connection with nature. This modern revival contributes to preserving Norse cultural heritage, allowing the wisdom and practices of the past to continue to inspire and guide us today.

THE SIGNIFICANCE OF THE WORLD TREE, YGGDRASIL

In the vast and intricate landscape of Norse mythology, Yggdrasil stands as a monumental pillar connecting all nine realms. This immense ash tree, often called the World Tree, is a profound symbol of life, death, and rebirth. Yggdrasil's branches stretch out into the heavens while its roots dive deep into the underworld, creating a bridge between the various realms that constitute the Norse cosmos. From Asgard, the realm of the gods, to Midgard, the world of humans, and even to Helheim, the land of the dead, Yggdrasil's reach is all-encompassing. It acts as the central axis around everything, embodying the interconnectedness of all life.

Yggdrasil teems with life and activity. At its roots gnaws the dragon Nidhogg, a fearsome creature that slowly eats away at the tree's foundation. Nidhogg's constant gnawing symbolizes the ever-present threat of decay and destruction, a reminder that even the mightiest structures are vulnerable. Atop Yggdrasil sits a majestic eagle, its piercing eyes scanning the realms. Between the eagle and Nidhogg runs the squirrel Ratatoskr, a mischievous messenger who carries insults and gossip between the two. This dynamic interaction among the inhabitants of Yggdrasil reflects the ongoing struggle and balance between opposing forces in the universe.

At the base of Yggdrasil lie three sacred wells, each with its own significance. The Well of Urd, guarded by the Norns, who are the fates of Norse mythology, is a source of wisdom and destiny. These three sisters—Urd, Verdandi, and Skuld—control the past, present, and future, weaving the destinies of gods and men alike. The Well of Mimir, another wellspring of wisdom, is where Odin sacrificed an eye to gain unparalleled knowledge. Finally, the Well of Hvergelmir, a source of primal waters, represents the very origin of life and the cyclical nature of existence.

One of the most significant myths involving Yggdrasil is Odin's self-sacrifice to gain knowledge of the runes. In his relentless quest for wisdom, Odin hanged himself from Yggdrasil's branches for nine days and nights, wounded by his own spear. This harrowing ordeal was a ritual of death and rebirth, culminating in the revelation of the runes, ancient symbols of power and knowledge. Odin's sacrifice underscores the profound connection between suffering, wisdom, and the cyclical nature of life. It also highlights Yggdrasil's role as a source of mystical knowledge and spiritual growth.

Yggdrasil also plays a pivotal role in the events of Ragnarok, the prophesied end of the world. As the cosmic battle unfolds, Yggdrasil trembles, its roots and branches shaking under the strain of the cataclysm. This upheaval signifies the end of the current world order and the beginning of a new cycle. Even as the old world is consumed by fire and water, Yggdrasil endures, a testimony to the continuity of life and the eternal cycle of destruction and rebirth. The tree's survival after Ragnarok symbolizes hope and renewal, promising that life will persist even in the face of overwhelming chaos.

In essence, Yggdrasil is the heart of Norse cosmology, a living symbol of the interwoven fate of gods, humans, and the cosmos. Its branches and roots touch every aspect of existence, reflecting the intricate balance and interconnectedness that define the Norse understanding of the world. Yggdrasil's enduring presence through cycles of creation and destruction underscores the timeless nature of these ancient beliefs, offering insights into the resilience and continuity of life.

RUNES: THEIR MEANINGS AND MAGICAL USES

Runes hold a special place in Norse mythology, both as an alphabet and as powerful symbols imbued with magic. The origins of runes are steeped in the legend of Odin, the Allfather, who was willing to endure great sacrifice to unlock their secrets. According to myth, Odin hung himself from the branches of Yggdrasil, the World Tree, for nine days and nights. Pierced by his own spear and denied food and drink, Odin suffered greatly. This act was a ritual of self-punishment and a profound quest for wisdom. On the ninth night, the runes revealed themselves to him, granting him the knowledge and power he sought. This moment marked the birth of runes as more than mere letters, transforming them into potent symbols of magic and prophecy.

The runic alphabet evolved over time, with variations that reflect the linguistic and cultural shifts in Norse society. The earliest and most well-known of these alphabets is the Elder Futhark, consisting of 24 characters. Each rune in this set is unique, carrying a phonetic value and a deeper symbolic meaning. For instance, the rune "Fehu," represented by a stylized "F," symbolizes wealth and abundance, reflecting the importance of livestock and material gain in Norse culture. As time passed and the Norse language evolved, the Elder Futhark gave way to the Younger Futhark. This later alphabet, with only sixteen characters, was more streamlined and adapted to the linguistic needs of the Viking Age.

Each rune in the alphabet carries its unique meaning, often connected to aspects of daily life and the natural world. The rune "Algiz," for example, symbolizes protection and defense. Its shape, resembling an elk's antlers, conveys a sense of strength and guardianship. "Ehwaz," another significant rune, represents partnership and cooperation. Depicted as a pair of horses, it underscores the importance of harmony and teamwork.

Runes were also used in various magical practices, serving as tools for divination and protection. One common use was rune casting, a form of divination where runes were drawn or cast onto a surface to interpret their meanings. Each rune's position and relationship to others provided insights and guidance, helping individuals make decisions or foresee future events. For example, a spread might reveal obstacles ahead or suggest favorable conditions for a particular endeavor.

Runes were also carved onto amulets and weapons, imbuing them with magical properties. An amulet inscribed with the rune "Algiz" would serve as a protective charm, warding off harm and evil spirits. Weapons adorned with runes were believed to enhance their strength and effectiveness in battle. The combination of runes and their placement on objects played a role in their magical potency. For instance, a sword with the rune "Tiwaz," symbolizing bravery and sacrifice, would inspire its wielder with courage and determination.

Runes also played a role in rituals and ceremonies. They were often carved into stones placed around sacred sites or inscribed on ritual tools to enhance their power. These inscriptions served as a bridge between the mortal and the divine, channeling the energy of the runes to achieve desired outcomes. The act of carving runes was itself a ritual, requiring precision and intent to ensure their proper activation.

The knowledge of runes, passed down through generations, held a revered place in Norse society. Rune masters, skilled in the art of reading and inscribing these symbols, were highly respected for their wisdom and magical abilities. Their expertise was sought in matters ranging from personal guidance to community decisions. The legacy of runes continues to captivate modern audiences, their mystical allure and symbolic depth offering a timeless connection to the ancient Norse world.

VIKING FUNERALS AND THE JOURNEY TO VALHALLA

Imagine standing by the shores of a fjord, the sun dipping below the horizon, casting a golden glow on a longship ready for its final voyage. Viking funerals were rich with symbolism and customs, reflecting the Norse belief in honoring the dead and ensuring their safe passage to the afterlife. The preparation of the body was meticulous and reverent. The deceased was washed, dressed in their finest clothes, and adorned with grave goods. These items, ranging from weapons and jewelry to everyday tools, were believed to assist the deceased in the afterlife. The inclusion of these goods was a testament to the Norse belief in the continuity of life beyond death.

Burial mounds, known as howes, were constructed as final resting places for the deceased. These mounds, often situated on elevated ground, served as lasting monuments to the departed. In some cases, ship burials were conducted, where the deceased was placed in a longship, surrounded by their possessions, and covered with stones and earth. The ship, a symbol of the journey to the afterlife, underscored the significance of the deceased's voyage to the next world. These burials were grand affairs, marked by rituals to honor the dead and secure their place in the afterlife.

The funeral rites held deep cultural and spiritual significance. They were about saying goodbye and ensuring the deceased's safe journey to the afterlife. Funeral pyres, where the body was cremated, played a central role in these rites. The flames symbolized purification and transformation, releasing the soul from its earthly bonds. Depending on local customs, the ashes were then collected and placed in an urn or scattered.

The journey to Valhalla, the hall of the slain, was a central aspect of Viking beliefs about the afterlife. Valhalla, ruled by Odin, was reserved for warriors who had died bravely in battle. The Valkyries, Odin's warrior maidens, selected these fallen heroes and guided them to Valhalla. Once there, the warriors, known as Einherjar, spent their days honing their combat skills and their nights feasting in Odin's great hall. This endless cycle of training and celebration was in preparation for Ragnarok, the prophesied end of the world, where the Einherjar would fight alongside the gods in the final battle.

One of the most poignant myths involving Viking funerals is the story of Baldr's death. As you probably remember, Baldr, the beloved god of light, was killed by a dart of mistletoe orchestrated by Loki. The gods, stricken with grief, prepared a grand funeral for Baldr. His body was placed on a majestic ship, Hringhorni, which was set ablaze and pushed out to sea. This funeral pyre, burning brightly against the night sky, was a powerful symbol of Baldr's journey to the afterlife. The gods' attempts to ransom Baldr from the underworld further illustrated the depth of their sorrow and the significance of funeral rites in honoring the dead.

Another notable example is the burial of ship burials. These burials were for the elite and common warriors who had distinguished themselves in battle. The deceased were laid in a ship, surrounded by their possessions, and covered with earth and stones. This practice reflected the Norse belief in the journey to the afterlife, where the ship symbolized the vessel that carried the soul to the next world. The grandeur of these burials underscored the importance of the deceased's status and achievements, ensuring they were honored appropriately.

Viking funerals expressed the Norse worldview, where life and death were deeply connected. The customs and rituals associated with these funerals were designed to honor the deceased, ensure their safe passage to the afterlife, and reinforce the social bonds within the community. Whether through the construction of burial mounds, the use of grave goods, or the grand spectacle of ship burials, these practices reflected the Norse belief in the continuity of life beyond death.

THE ROLE OF SKALDS AND ORAL TRADITION

Imagine a night in a Viking longhouse, the fire crackling and shadows dancing on the walls as a Skald begins his tale. Skalds were the poets and historians of Norse society, revered for their ability to weave words into stories that preserved the culture and history of their people. They were custodians of the collective memory, ensuring that the deeds of gods and heroes were remembered and passed down through generations. In a world where written records were scarce, the Skalds' role was essential. They kept the oral traditions alive, narrating sagas and epics that conveyed the values, beliefs, and history of the Norse people.

Skaldic poetry was marked by its intricate techniques and unique styles. One of the most notable features was the use of kennings—metaphorical expressions that replaced simple nouns. For example, a ship might be called a "sea-steed" or "wave-horse," adding a layer of imagery and meaning to the poem. Alliteration was another key element, where the initial consonant sounds of words were repeated to create a rhythmic flow. Skalds also employed complex meters and structures, making their verses challenging to compose and captivating to hear. These poetic conventions were artistic choices and tools that helped the Skalds remember and recite long and intricate narratives.

In Norse culture, oral tradition was important. Before the advent of written texts like the Eddas, stories, myths, and historical events were transmitted orally. This method of storytelling ensured that the wisdom and experiences of the past were preserved and accessible to future generations. Skalds played a vital role in this process, acting as both performers and educators. Their recitations were communal events that brought people together, fostering a shared cultural identity. The oral tradition also allowed for flexibility and adaptation, enabling the stories to evolve while retaining their core essence.

Famous examples of Skaldic poetry highlight the talent and significance of these wordsmiths. Egil Skallagrimsson, a renowned Skald, composed poems that reflected the trials and triumphs of his life. His poetry, rich with emotion and imagery, addressed themes like loss, honor, and vengeance. One of his most famous works, *Sonatorrek*, mourns the death of his son and showcases his mastery of poetic form and deep emotional resonance. The preservation of heroic sagas, such as the legendary deeds of Sigurd and the Völsungs, also owes much to the oral tradition maintained by Skalds. These narratives influenced Norse literature and later literary traditions, leaving an indelible mark on the cultural landscape.

The Skalds' role extended beyond just storytelling. They were also advisors and chroniclers, often serving at the courts of kings and chieftains. Their poems could immortalize the deeds of their patrons, ensuring that their names and actions were remembered long after their deaths. This relationship between the Skalds and their patrons was symbiotic; the Skalds gained protection and patronage, while the patrons gained immortality through verse. The power of the spoken word in Norse society was profound, shaping perceptions and influencing actions.

In essence, Skalds and the oral tradition were pillars of Norse culture. They captured the spirit of their times, preserving the legacy of their people through the art of storytelling. Their verses, filled with vivid imagery and wisdom, continue to inspire and educate, offering a window into the world of the ancient Norse. As we explore these traditions, we gain a deeper appreciation for the richness and complexity of Norse mythology and the enduring power of the spoken word.

In the next chapter, we will explore the fascinating world of Norse mythology in modern culture, examining how these ancient stories continue to influence and inspire contemporary literature, movies, and more.

7

NORSE MYTHOLOGY IN MODERN CULTURE

Have you ever found yourself lost in a book, only to realize the story's roots stretch back to ancient myths? Norse mythology has a remarkable ability to weave itself into the fabric of modern literature, creating rich, compelling narratives that captivate readers of all ages. The timeless tales of gods, heroes, and mythical creatures continue to inspire contemporary authors, making Norse mythology as relevant today as it was centuries ago.

NORSE MYTHOLOGY IN MODERN LITERATURE

Norse mythology has left an indelible mark on modern literature, influencing some of the most beloved and enduring stories of our time. J.R.R. Tolkien's The Lord of the Rings is a prime example of this impact. Tolkien, a scholar of ancient languages and myths, drew heavily from Norse mythology to create his rich, immersive world. The dwarves of Middle-earth, with their intricate runes and names like Gimli and Thorin, are directly inspired by the dwarves of Norse lore. Tolkien's use of runes, similar to the Norse Elder Futhark, adds an authentic layer to his world-building, making Middle-earth feel like a place steeped in ancient history and magic. The epic quests, the battle between good and evil, and the presence of wise, enigmatic characters like Gandalf are all reminiscent of the grand narratives found in Norse mythology.

Neil Gaiman's *Norse Mythology* offers a fresh retelling of classic Norse myths, bringing the stories of Odin, Thor, and Loki to a contemporary audience. Gaiman's prose breathes new life into these ancient tales, making them accessible and engaging for modern readers. His book captures the essence of Norse mythology while adding his unique narrative flair, ensuring that the legends remain vibrant and relevant. Each story in Gaiman's collection delves into the complex relationships and adventures of the gods, highlighting their timeless appeal and the universal themes they embody.

For younger readers, Rick Riordan's Magnus Chase and the Gods of Asgard series introduces Norse mythology through the eyes of a modern teenager. Riordan, known for his Percy Jackson series, brings the world of Norse gods and mythical creatures to life in a fun and educational way. The protagonist, Magnus Chase, discovers he is the son of a Norse god, leading him on a series of thrilling adventures. Riordan's books are filled with humor, action, and relatable characters, making ancient myths accessible to a new generation. By blending contemporary settings with mythological elements, Riordan ensures that young readers can connect with the stories and learn about Norse mythology in an engaging way.

Norse themes and motifs are prevalent in fantasy literature, reflecting the rich narrative tradition of these ancient myths. The concept of heroism and the epic quest is a cornerstone of Norse mythology, evident in the tales of gods and heroes who embark on perilous journeys to achieve great deeds. This theme resonates in modern fantasy, where protagonists often undertake quests that test their courage, strength, and morality. The portrayal of gods, giants, and mythical creatures also draws heavily from Norse mythology, providing a wealth of inspiration for authors. These beings, with their complex personalities and powers, add depth and intrigue to fantasy worlds and make the stories more compelling.

Norse mythology's impact extends beyond fantasy into other literary genres, including science fiction and horror. In science fiction, the idea of exploring different realms and encountering gods and mythical beings can be seen in works that blend high-tech settings with ancient myths. Horror literature also draws from Norse mythology, using its darker elements to create chilling narratives. The themes of chaos, destruction, and the supernatural present in Norse myths provide rich material for horror stories, adding depth and historical context to the terror.

Academic works continue to explore Norse mythology, furthering our understanding of these ancient stories and their cultural significance. Comparative mythology studies examine the similarities and differences between Norse myths and those of other cultures, shedding light on the universal themes that connect humanity. Interdisciplinary research connects Norse myths to history and anthropology, exploring how these stories reflect the beliefs, values, and experiences of the Norse people. This scholarly exploration ensures that Norse mythology remains a vibrant field of study, contributing to our broader understanding of human culture and history.

Norse mythology's influence on modern literature is vast and varied, enriching the stories we tell and the worlds we imagine. It offers timeless themes, complex characters, and rich narratives that continue to captivate and inspire. Whether through epic quests, retellings of ancient myths, or explorations of fate and destiny, the legacy of Norse mythology endures, weaving its way into the hearts and minds of readers worldwide.

THE INFLUENCE OF NORSE MYTHS IN MOVIES AND TV SHOWS

Norse mythology has found a new home on the big screen, captivating audiences with tales of gods, heroes, and epic battles. Marvel's Thor series is a prime example, bringing the thunder god and his mischievous brother Loki into the modern age. These films blend ancient myths with contemporary storytelling, creating a universe where Norse gods interact with humans and other superheroes. Thor, portrayed by Chris Hemsworth, retains his iconic hammer, Mjölnir, and his warrior spirit, while Loki, played by Tom Hiddleston, embodies the trickster's cunning and charm. The series has introduced millions to Norse mythology, making these ancient tales accessible and exciting for a global audience.

Another notable film is *The 13th Warrior*, based on Michael Crichton's novel *Eaters of the Dead*. This movie follows a Muslim ambassador, played by Antonio Banderas, who joins a group of Vikings to combat a mysterious and deadly threat. Directed by John McTiernan, the film blends historical elements with Norse mythology, showcasing the bravery and resilience of Viking warriors. The portrayal of Viking culture, with its emphasis on honor and heroism, resonates deeply with the themes found in Norse myths.

The influence of Norse mythology also extends to the Lord of the Rings film trilogy, where J.R.R. Tolkien's love for these ancient stories shines through. While various mythological sources primarily inspire Tolkien's work, the presence of Norse elements is undeniable. From the dwarves with their runic inscriptions to the epic battles that mirror the grand conflicts of Norse sagas, the films capture the essence of these ancient tales. The sense of fate and destiny that permeates the trilogy echoes the themes found in Norse mythology, creating a rich, immersive experience for viewers.

Television has also embraced Norse mythology, with several series bringing these ancient stories to life. The History Channel's *Vikings* is a standout example, blending historical and mythological elements to tell the saga of Ragnar Lothbrok and his descendants. The series dives into the lives of Viking warriors, their explorations, and their interactions with gods and mythical beings. By weaving historical facts with mythological themes, *Vikings* offers a compelling portrayal of Norse culture and beliefs.

Netflix's *Ragnarok* takes a different approach, setting the story in a modern-day Norwegian town. The series follows a teenage boy, Magne, who discovers he is the reincarnation of Thor. As he grapples with his newfound identity, he must confront ancient enemies and modern issues, such as industrial pollution. *Ragnarok* cleverly merges contemporary challenges with Norse mythology, creating a relevant and timeless narrative. The show's reinterpretation of Norse gods and themes resonates with younger audiences, making these ancient stories accessible and engaging.

American Gods, adapted from Neil Gaiman's novel, features Norse gods adapting to modern society. The series, which follows Shadow Moon in a conflict between Old Gods and New Gods, portrays Norse deities like Odin and Loki in a contemporary context. This juxtaposition of ancient and modern highlights the enduring relevance of Norse mythology, exploring how these timeless stories can adapt and survive in a changing world. The complex characters and intricate plotlines draw viewers into a world where myth and reality collide, offering a fresh perspective on Norse myths.

Filmmakers often balance mythological fidelity with creative storytelling, blending historical facts with mythical elements to create engaging narratives. For example, Marvel's *Thor* series takes significant creative liberties, reimagining characters and events to fit within the Marvel Cinematic Universe. While the essence of the myths remains, the adaptations are tailored to resonate with modern audiences. Similarly, *The 13th Warrior* and *Ragnarok* reinterpret Norse themes to suit their unique narratives, blending historical accuracy with imaginative storytelling.

This creative blending allows filmmakers to explore Norse mythology while making it accessible to contemporary viewers. By reinterpreting characters and events, they highlight the timeless appeal of these ancient stories. The cultural impact of these adaptations is profound, sparking a resurgence of interest in Norse myths and Viking history. Symbols and themes from Norse mythology, such as Thor's hammer or the concept of Ragnarok, have become ingrained in mainstream media, influencing how we perceive these ancient tales.

Through movies and TV shows, Norse mythology continues to captivate and inspire, bridging the gap between ancient and modern myth and reality.

NORSE THEMES IN VIDEO GAMES

Video games have a unique way of bringing ancient myths to life, offering players an immersive experience where they can explore the realms of gods and monsters. Norse mythology, specifically, has found a special place in the gaming world. Game developers have skillfully woven these myths into their narratives, allowing players to interact with Norse gods, battle mythical creatures, and traverse landscapes inspired by ancient lore. Integrating Norse mythology into video games is about building a world where players can live out the epic quests and heroic journeys that define these ancient tales.

One of the standout titles that deeply explores Norse mythology is *God of War* (2018). This game takes players on a journey through the nine realms, guided by Kratos, a Spartan warrior, and his son, Atreus. The game intricately blends Norse myths with its own lore, featuring gods like Odin, Thor, and Baldur. The landscapes are meticulously designed to reflect the mythological settings, from the frozen wastes of Midgard to the fiery depths of Muspelheim. Instead of just using Norse mythology as a backdrop, the developers explored the complexities of these myths, presenting characters with depth and nuance. This approach allows players to experience the myths in an authentic and engaging way.

Assassin's Creed Valhalla is another game that brings Norse mythology to the forefront. Set during the Viking Age, players take on the role of Eivor, a Viking warrior exploring England. The game masterfully incorporates elements of Norse culture and mythology into its narrative. Players can visit Asgard, interact with gods like Odin, and witness the grandeur of the Bifrost Bridge. The game's attention to historical detail and mythological elements provides a rich, immersive experience. It offers a unique blend of history and myth, allowing players to explore the Viking world in all its complexity.

Hellblade: Senua's Sacrifice takes a different approach by exploring the psychological and cosmological aspects of Norse mythology. The game follows Senua, a Pict warrior, on a harrowing journey to Helheim to rescue the soul of her dead lover. Along the way, she battles Norse gods and giants, all while grappling with her own mental illness. The game's portrayal of Norse cosmology is haunting and beautiful, drawing players into a world where the lines between reality and myth are blurred. This game stands out for its emotional depth and innovative use of mythology to explore themes of grief and redemption.

The Banner Saga trilogy offers a more traditional take on Norse-inspired storytelling. This tactical role-playing game series draws heavily from Norse aesthetics and mythology. Players lead a caravan of warriors and civilians across a dying world, facing both human and mythical threats. The game's art style and storytelling are deeply influenced by Norse sagas, creating a timeless and epic narrative. The presence of gods, giants, and mystical creatures adds complexity to the storyline, making each decision feel weighty and significant.

Video games offer an immersive experience that allows players to explore Norse mythology interactively. Unlike traditional media, games enable players to engage with the myths on a personal level, making choices that influence the story's outcome. This interactivity enhances the educational potential of video games, turning them into powerful tools for mythological education. Players don't just read about the myths; they live them, gaining a deeper appreciation for the stories and their cultural significance.

The rich narratives found in games like *God of War, Assassin's Creed Valhalla, Hellblade: Senua's Sacrifice* and *The Banner Saga* serve as both entertainment and education. They introduce players to the complexities of Norse mythology, highlighting the timeless themes and motifs that continue to resonate. By allowing players to step into the shoes of heroes, interact with gods, and explore mythological landscapes, these games provide a unique and engaging way to experience the ancient tales of Norse mythology.

THE MODERN REVIVAL OF NORSE PAGANISM

In recent years, there's been a noticeable resurgence in Norse paganism, often referred to as Ásatrú or Heathenry. This revival stems from a deep-seated desire to reconnect with ancient spiritual practices and cultural heritage.

One of the key aspects of modern Norse paganism is the celebration of ancient rituals, such as Blót and other seasonal festivals. Blót, a sacrificial ritual, is a central practice where offerings are made to gods, spirits, and ancestors. These rituals, which may involve sacrificing animals, food, or drink, are held to honor the divine and seek blessings. Seasonal festivals, like Yule and Midsummer, mark important points in the agricultural calendar and celebrate the cycles of nature. These gatherings are spiritual and communal, encouraging a sense of unity among participants.

Modern Norse pagans also incorporate runes and Seidr into their spiritual practices. Runes, the ancient alphabet used by the Norse, are often employed in divination and magical workings. Each rune carries specific meanings and powers, allowing practitioners to seek guidance and insight. Seidr, a form of Norse shamanism, involves trance work, chanting, and rituals to connect with the spiritual realm. Practitioners of Seidr, known as Seidrworkers or Volva, use these techniques to gain knowledge, heal, and perform magic. These practices connect modern pagans to the mystical aspects of their ancient traditions.

Communities and organizations play a significant role in the modern revival of Norse paganism. Groups like Ásatrúarfélagið in Iceland have been instrumental in promoting and preserving these ancient practices. Founded in 1972, Ásatrúarfélagið aims to revive the old ways and provide a community for those who follow the Norse gods. They organize rituals, educational events, and seasonal celebrations, creating a supportive network for practitioners. Online communities and forums also connect modern pagans worldwide, allowing them to share knowledge, experiences, and support. These digital spaces foster a sense of global community, making it easier for individuals to practice and learn about Norse paganism.

The cultural and social impact of the modern revival of Norse paganism is multifaceted. In media and popular culture, Norse paganism is often romanticized and depicted as a mystical and intriguing belief system. This portrayal has contributed to the growing interest in ancient Norse practices. However, modern practitioners face challenges as well. Misconceptions and stereotypes about paganism can lead to misunderstandings and prejudice. Despite these obstacles, many find that the revival of Norse paganism offers opportunities for personal growth, spiritual fulfillment, and cultural preservation.

Contemporary Norse pagans often navigate a complex landscape of tradition and modernity. They strive to honor the old ways while adapting them to contemporary life. This balance is reflected in the diverse practices and beliefs within the community. Some focus on historical accuracy, seeking to replicate ancient rituals as closely as possible. Others take a more eclectic approach, blending traditional elements with modern spiritual practices. This diversity allows for a rich and dynamic expression of Norse paganism, accommodating a wide range of beliefs and practices.

NORSE MYTHOLOGY AND HEAVY METAL MUSIC

Have you ever wondered why heavy metal music often feels like an epic saga of gods, warriors, and ancient battles? The connection between Norse mythology and heavy metal is deeply rooted in the genre's appeal to epic and heroic themes. Norse mythology, with its larger-than-life gods, fierce battles, and tales of valor, provides the perfect backdrop for the grandeur and intensity of heavy metal. The genre thrives on powerful imagery and dramatic narratives, elements that are abundantly present in Norse myths.

One of the most striking aspects of this connection is the use of Norse symbols and imagery in band names and album art. Bands often draw from the rich tapestry of Norse mythology to craft their identities, using symbols like Mjölnir (Thor's hammer) and runic inscriptions to evoke a sense of ancient power and mysticism. Album covers frequently depict scenes of Viking warriors, majestic longships, and mythical creatures, transporting listeners to a world where the lines between history and myth blur. This visual connection enhances the thematic depth of the music, creating a cohesive experience that resonates with fans.

Amon Amarth is one band that has masterfully incorporated Viking-themed lyrics into their music. Their songs often tell stories of legendary battles, heroic deeds, and the harsh realities of Viking life. Tracks like "Twilight of the Thunder God" and "Guardians of Asgaard" are filled with references to Norse gods and epic confrontations, bringing the myths to life through powerful, aggressive music. The band's dedication to Norse themes has earned them a loyal following, drawing fans who are captivated by the raw energy and historical depth of their lyrics.

Bathory, another influential band, has significantly contributed to the genre with albums like *Hammerheart* and *Twilight of the Gods*. These albums are seminal works in the Viking metal subgenre, blending heavy metal with themes of Norse mythology and paganism. Bathory's music often explores the spiritual and existential aspects of the myths, like the gods' roles and the cyclical nature of existence. Their work has inspired countless other bands to explore similar themes, solidifying their place as pioneers in the genre.

Enslaved is a band that seamlessly incorporates Norse mythology into their music, combining black metal with progressive elements to create a unique sound. Their lyrics often talk about the cosmology and philosophy of Norse myths, exploring themes of creation, destruction, and transformation. Albums like *Eld* and *Frost* are rich with references to ancient myths and legends, offering listeners a deep and immersive experience. Enslaved's music entertains and educates, providing insights into the complex and multifaceted world of Norse mythology.

Manowar's song "The Sons of Odin" is another example of how Norse mythology has influenced heavy metal. The track celebrates the warrior culture and heroic deeds of the Norse gods, capturing the essence of their strength and valor. Manowar's music often glorifies the heroic ideals found in Norse myths, emphasizing themes of honor, bravery, and loyalty. This celebration of warrior culture resonates deeply with fans, inspiring a sense of unity and pride.

Norse-themed metal music has had a significant cultural impact, influencing fans' understanding and appreciation of Norse mythology. The genre has played a role in popularizing these ancient myths, making them accessible to a broader audience. Through their music, bands create a community and subculture that celebrates Norse heritage and mythology. Fans often embrace the symbols, rituals, and values depicted in the songs, fostering a sense of connection and identity. This cultural phenomenon extends beyond music, influencing everything from fashion to literature and ensuring that the legacy of Norse mythology continues to thrive in the modern world.

NORSE SYMBOLS IN CONTEMPORARY ART AND FASHION

Norse symbols have found a vibrant place in modern art, where contemporary artists often incorporate imagery from Viking culture and mythology. This revival of Viking art styles in modern works is an aesthetic choice and a way to connect with the ancient past. Artists like Johan Egerkrans have made significant contributions by depicting scenes from Norse myths with meticulous detail and a modern flair. Egerkrans' illustrations bring to life the gods, giants, and mythical creatures of Norse mythology, capturing their essence while making them accessible to a contemporary audience. His works often feature dramatic, dynamic compositions that draw viewers into the mythological world.

Runes and mythological figures also play a significant role in visual art, serving as powerful symbols with deep meanings. Runes, the ancient alphabet used by the Norse, are often depicted in modern artworks to evoke a sense of mystery and ancient wisdom. These symbols are imbued with the same power and significance they held in ancient times.

Tattoo artists have also embraced Norse symbols, using them to create intricate and meaningful designs. Tattoos featuring runes, Yggdrasil (the World Tree), and other mythological motifs have become increasingly popular. These designs are more than just body art; they are expressions of personal identity. Many people choose Norse symbols for their tattoos because they resonate with the values and stories of the myths. The permanence of tattoos adds another layer of significance, making the symbols a lasting part of the individual's life.

In fashion, Norse imagery has gained popularity in clothing and accessories, bringing ancient symbols into everyday wear. Viking-themed jewelry, such as Thor's hammer pendants and bracelets adorned with runes, has become a fashion statement. These pieces often carry a sense of strength and protection, reflecting the qualities associated with the gods and heroes they represent. Clothing lines have also incorporated Norse motifs, with designs featuring intricate knotwork, mythological scenes, and runic inscriptions. These elements add a unique, historical touch to modern fashion, allowing people to carry a piece of Norse mythology with them.

Moreover, the appeal of Norse symbols lies in their timelessness and universality. The stories and values they represent—courage, wisdom, loyalty, and the eternal struggle between order and chaos —are as relevant today as they were in ancient times. These symbols transcend cultural boundaries, resonating with people from diverse backgrounds. They remind us of the enduring power of myth and how ancient stories continue to shape our modern world.

In conclusion, Norse symbols in contemporary art and fashion offer a fascinating blend of the ancient and the modern. They connect us to a rich cultural heritage while allowing for personal expression and identity. Whether through visual art, tattoos, jewelry, or clothing, these symbols continue to captivate and inspire, reminding us of the timeless nature of Norse mythology and its ongoing influence on our lives.

The enduring appeal of Norse mythology in modern culture highlights its impact on art, literature, entertainment, and spirituality. As we explore further, we'll see how these ancient stories continue to shape and inspire new generations, powerfully bridging the past and the present. Next, we'll discover the broader impact of Norse mythology on global cultural traditions and its relevance in today's world.

8

COMPARATIVE MYTHOLOGY AND GLOBAL IMPACT

Have you ever considered how different cultures have shaped their understanding of the world through myth? The stories of gods and heroes from Norse and Greek mythology have similarities and fascinating contrasts. These myths have sculpted their respective cultures and left a lasting impact on how we interpret the human experience. Exploring these parallels and divergences can deepen your appreciation for the rich tapestry of human storytelling.

NORSE VS. GREEK MYTHOLOGY: PARALLELS AND CONTRASTS

When comparing the pantheons of Norse and Greek mythology, one finds striking similarities and distinct differences. The Norse gods, known as the Aesir, and the Greek gods, known as the Olympians, each inhabit a divine realm—Asgard and Olympus, respectively. Both pantheons are led by powerful chief gods. As you know, Odin, the Allfather of the Norse gods, is a complex figure associated with wisdom, war, and death. He sacrificed his eye for wisdom and hung himself on Yggdrasil, the World Tree, to gain knowledge of runes. Zeus, the king of the Greek gods, rules over the sky and wields thunderbolts. Unlike Odin's multifaceted nature, Zeus primarily focuses on maintaining order and justice among the gods and humans. Both deities embody leadership and power but reflect the distinct values of their cultures: wisdom and sacrifice for the Norse and authority and justice for the Greeks.

The creation myths of these two traditions reveal different approaches to explaining the origins of the world. In Norse mythology, the cosmos began with Ginnungagap, a vast primordial void. From this void, the realms of fire (Muspelheim) and ice (Niflheim) emerged, and their interaction birthed Ymir, the first giant. The gods Odin, Vili, and Vé later killed Ymir, using his body to create the world—his flesh became the earth, his blood the seas, his bones the mountains, and his skull the sky. This act of creation through destruction underscores the Norse theme of cyclical renewal.

In contrast, Greek mythology describes the world's creation through the union of the primordial deities Gaia (Earth) and Uranus (Sky). Their offspring, the Titans, eventually gave rise to the Olympian gods. The Greek creation myth emphasizes a more orderly progression from chaos to cosmos, reflecting a structured universe emerging from primordial origins.

Fate and prophecy play roles in both mythologies but manifest differently. Norse mythology is deeply intertwined with the concept of Ragnarok, the prophesied end of the world. This cataclysmic event is inevitable; even the gods know their impending doom. The Greek concept of fate, personified by the Moirai (Fates), also dictates the destinies of gods and mortals alike.

However, Greek myths often focus on individual prophecies and the struggle to alter or accept one's fate. Heroes like Oedipus and Achilles grapple with their destinies, highlighting themes of personal choice and inevitable consequences.

Heroic journeys and trials are central to both mythological traditions, showcasing the enduring human spirit. In Norse mythology, Sigurd is a quintessential hero, renowned for slaying the dragon Fafnir and gaining wisdom through tasting the dragon's heart. His quest is a blend of bravery, cunning, and tragic fate. Similarly, the Greek hero Heracles (Hercules) undertakes twelve labors, each a monumental task that tests his strength, intelligence, and endurance. Both heroes embody the virtues of their cultures—Sigurd's wisdom and Heracles' strength. The trials of Odysseus on his long journey home from the Trojan War parallel the challenges faced by Thor and Loki in their adventures. Odysseus' cunning and resilience mirror Thor's brute strength and Loki's cleverness, highlighting the diverse qualities valued by the Greeks and Norse.

These comparisons highlight how Norse and Greek mythologies, while distinct, share common themes that resonate with the human experience. By examining these myths, you can better appreciate the rich cultural tapestries they weave and the universal truths they reveal about humanity.

NORSE INFLUENCE ON J.R.R. TOLKIEN'S MIDDLE-EARTH

J.R.R. Tolkien's deep fascination with Norse mythology shaped his creation of Middle-earth. If you have ever read *The Silmarillion*, you might have noticed the echoes of Norse myths resonating through its pages. Much like the Norse *Eddas*, which chronicle the birth and fate of the cosmos, *The Silmarillion* recounts the world's creation and its inhabitants' epic tales. The storytelling style in both works is grand and sweeping, filled with heroic deeds, tragic destinies, and the eternal struggle between good and evil. Tolkien's universe, much like the Norse cosmos, is a place where the gods (or Valar) shape the world and where the fate of all beings is intertwined with cosmic events.

The characters and creatures in Tolkien's works draw heavily from Norse mythology. Take Gandalf, for instance. He bears a striking resemblance to Odin, the Allfather. Both are wise, wandering figures who guide and mentor heroes. Gandalf's journey through Middle-earth, offering counsel and aid, mirrors Odin's travels through the Nine Realms, seeking wisdom and knowledge. The dwarves of Middle-earth are another clear example of Norse influence. They are master craftsmen, much like their Norse counterparts, who forged powerful items such as Thor's hammer Mjölnir. Tolkien's dwarves, with their love of mining and craftsmanship, are directly inspired by the Norse myths, where dwarves are integral to the creation of magical artifacts.

Themes and motifs in Tolkien's Middle-earth also bear the imprint of Norse mythology. The concept of heroic sacrifice and fate is a recurring theme in both. Consider the story of Aragorn, who accepts his destiny as king, much like the Norse heroes who embrace their fates, even when it leads to their doom. The epic battles in The Lord of the Rings echo the grand conflicts of Norse myths, such as the final battle of Ragnarok. These themes highlight the struggle between good and evil, the importance of bravery, and the inevitability of destiny, all central to both Norse mythology and Tolkien's narratives.

The linguistic influence of Old Norse on Tolkien's created languages is another fascinating aspect. Tolkien, a philologist by profession, was deeply inspired by Old Norse when crafting the languages of Middle-earth. The Elvish languages, particularly Sindarin and Quenya, contain elements derived from Old Norse. Names and terms from Norse mythology are woven into the fabric of Tolkien's world. For example, the dwarves' names in *The Hobbit*, such as Thorin Oakenshield, come directly from *Völuspá*, a part of the *Poetic Edda*. This linguistic connection enriches the world of Middle-earth, grounding it in a tapestry of ancient myth and language.

One of the most striking parallels is the story of the One Ring, which draws inspiration from the cursed ring Andvaranaut in Norse legend. The tale of Andvaranaut, a powerful ring that brings misfortune to its bearer, clearly influenced Tolkien's creation of the One Ring, which corrupts and ensnares those who possess it. This motif of a powerful yet cursed object is a recurring theme in both Norse mythology and Tolkien's work, symbolizing the dangerous allure of power and the inevitable downfall it brings.

Tolkien's deep connection to Norse mythology is further evidenced by his involvement with the Leeds Viking Club and his scholarly work on Norse texts. His knowledge and appreciation of these ancient myths allowed him to create a world that feels both familiar and fantastical. By blending elements of Norse mythology with his imagination, Tolkien crafted stories that resonate with timeless themes of heroism, sacrifice, and the eternal struggle between light and darkness.

The influence of Norse mythology on Tolkien's Middle-earth is a testament to the enduring power of these ancient stories. They continue to inspire and captivate, weaving their way into the fabric of modern fantasy literature and offering readers a rich, immersive experience that bridges the ancient and the contemporary.

COMPARATIVE ANALYSIS OF CELTIC MYTHOLOGY

Exploring the pantheons of Norse and Celtic mythology reveals a fascinating world of gods and goddesses with both shared and distinct characteristics. The Norse pantheon, divided into the Aesir and Vanir, includes deities like Odin, Thor, and Freyja. These gods are known for their strength, wisdom, and, sometimes, human-like flaws. Odin, the Allfather, is a figure of immense power and knowledge. He is often depicted as a wise old man who sacrificed much to gain wisdom, including hanging himself on Yggdrasil, the World Tree.

In contrast, the Celtic pantheon, primarily the Tuatha Dé Danann, features gods and goddesses such as Lugh and Brigid, who are closely tied to aspects of daily life and nature. Lugh, a god of many skills, is often compared to Odin in terms of his versatility and importance. However, Lugh's domain includes arts, crafts, and warfare, reflecting a broader range of human activities. Brigid, another central figure, presides over healing, fertility, and poetry, showcasing the Celtic emphasis on the interconnectedness of life and creativity.

When it comes to creation myths and cosmology, both Norse and Celtic traditions offer rich, complex narratives. The Norse myth of Yggdrasil, the immense ash tree that connects all realms, serves as the axis of the universe. This tree's roots and branches link the heavens, earth, and underworld, symbolizing the interconnectedness of all life. Creation in Norse mythology begins with Ginnungagap, a primordial void, and the interaction between the realms of fire and ice, leading to the emergence of Ymir, the first giant. This chaotic beginning contrasts with the Celtic cosmology, which features its own sacred tree, often referred to as the World Tree, symbolizing life's axis. Celtic creation myths, however, are less centralized and more fragmented, focusing on the emergence of the Tuatha Dé Danann from the mist and their eventual settlement in Ireland. Both traditions emphasize the theme of creation from chaos and the importance of primordial beings, but the Norse myths are more structured in their cosmological hierarchy.

Heroism and the concept of the otherworld play pivotal roles in both mythologies. In Norse mythology, Valhalla is the hall of slain warriors, ruled by Odin, where heroes prepare for the final battle of Ragnarok. This afterlife reflects the Norse values of bravery and honor in combat. Heroes like Sigurd, who slays the dragon Fafnir, embody these qualities, undertaking epic quests that test their strength and wisdom.

In Celtic mythology, the otherworld, known as Tír na nÓg, is a mystical, eternal realm of youth and beauty. It is not reserved solely for warriors but is accessible to those who demonstrate exceptional qualities. Heroes like Cú Chulainn, renowned for his superhuman abilities and tragic fate, undertake quests that are as much about personal growth and moral challenges as they are about physical prowess. The otherworldly journeys in both mythologies highlight the cultural importance of heroism, though the Norse focus more on martial valor while the Celts emphasize a blend of physical and spiritual heroism.

Cultural and ritual practices in Norse and Celtic traditions also share intriguing similarities. The Norse used runes, an ancient alphabet imbued with magical properties, in their rituals and divination practices. These runes were carved into stones, weapons, and amulets, serving both practical and mystical purposes. In comparison, the Celts used Ogham, an early medieval alphabet, primarily for inscriptions and possibly for divination. Both traditions viewed their scripts as more than mere writing systems, attributing to them a sacred significance that bridged the mortal and divine realms. Seasonal festivals further illustrate the parallels between these cultures. The Norse celebrated Yule, a midwinter festival that honored the rebirth of the sun and involved feasting, sacrifices, and rituals to ensure the return of light and warmth.

Similarly, the Celts celebrated Samhain, marking the end of the harvest season and the beginning of winter. Samhain was a time when the veil between the worlds of the living and the dead was thin, allowing for communication with ancestors and spirits. These festivals reflect a shared reverence for nature's cycles and the importance of community and ritual in maintaining harmony with the natural world.

THE GLOBAL SPREAD OF VIKING LORE

Have you ever wondered how Viking culture spread across Europe and beyond, leaving an indelible mark on global history? The Vikings, known for their seafaring prowess, embarked on expeditions that reached far beyond their Scandinavian homelands. They established settlements in diverse regions, from the British Isles to the coasts of Greenland and Newfoundland. More than just military outposts, these were thriving communities engaged in trade, agriculture, and cultural exchange. In places like Dublin, York, and Normandy, Viking influence became deeply embedded in the local culture, shaping the development of these regions for centuries.

The Vikings were adept traders whose networks stretched from the Middle East to North America. They exchanged goods, stories, and cultural practices with other civilizations through trade. Items like amber, fur, and iron from the North found their way into distant markets, while silver, silk, and spices journeyed back to Scandinavia. This exchange enriched Viking culture and introduced new ideas and technologies. The legacy of Viking navigation and shipbuilding is particularly notable. Their longships, designed for both speed and durability, were marvels of engineering that allowed them to traverse vast distances and navigate open seas and shallow rivers. These ships facilitated exploration and conquest and symbolized the Vikings' connection to the sea and their adventurous spirit.

Viking lore has been a rich source of inspiration in global media, contributing to a romanticized image that often overshadows historical realities. Literature, films, and art have portrayed Vikings as fierce warriors and intrepid explorers, sometimes glossing over their roles as traders and settlers. Novels like *The Last Kingdom* series by Bernard Cornwell and movies such as *How to Train Your Dragon* capture the adventurous and often brutal aspects of Viking life. Television series like *Vikings* have brought these stories to a broad audience, blending historical events with dramatic flair. These portrayals emphasize the Vikings' bravery, complex social structures, and enduring legacy as one of history's most fascinating cultures.

The impact of Viking lore on modern cultural practices is evident in the resurgence of Viking festivals and reenactments. Communities worldwide celebrate their Viking heritage with events that include mock battles, traditional crafts, and storytelling. These festivals provide a way for people to connect with their ancestry and keep the spirit of Viking culture alive. Viking symbols, such as the Valknut and Mjölnir, have become popular motifs in modern art and fashion. These symbols, once used in religious and cultural contexts, now adorn everything from jewelry to tattoos, bridging the ancient and contemporary worlds.

Scholarly interest in Viking history and mythology remains strong, driven by ongoing research and archaeological discoveries.

Scholars study Viking sagas and historical texts to uncover insights into Norse society, beliefs, and everyday life. These texts, written centuries ago, continue to provide valuable information and inspire new interpretations. Archaeological excavations have unearthed Viking artifacts, settlements, and burial sites, shedding light on their craftsmanship, trade networks, and social structures. Discoveries such as the Oseberg and Gokstad ships offer a glimpse into the sophisticated shipbuilding techniques and the ceremonial significance of seafaring in Viking culture.

The academic exploration of Viking history also extends to understanding their myths and legends. With its rich tapestry of gods, heroes, and cosmic events, Norse mythology is a subject of fascination for historians, literary scholars, and enthusiasts alike. The study of these myths reveals the values, fears, and aspirations of the Norse people, providing a deeper understanding of their world. Institutions and museums dedicated to Viking history, such as the Viking Ship Museum in Oslo and the Jorvik Viking Centre in York, play an important role in preserving and disseminating this knowledge. Through exhibitions, educational programs, and interactive displays, they bring Viking history to life for visitors of all ages, ensuring that the legacy of the Vikings continues to inspire and educate.

NORSE MYTHOLOGY IN PSYCHOLOGICAL THEORY

Norse mythology has found a unique place in psychological theory, offering rich material for understanding the human psyche. One of the most fascinating applications is through archetypal analysis, a concept developed by Carl Jung. Archetypes are universal, symbolic images that appear across cultures and are embedded in our collective unconscious. In Norse mythology, gods and heroes embody these archetypes, providing a mirror to our inner selves. For example, Odin represents the wise old man, a figure of knowledge and guidance, while Thor embodies the hero archetype, symbolizing strength and protection. These characters resonate deeply within us, reflecting universal aspects of the human experience.

Jung's theories on the collective unconscious and archetypes have been influenced by mythological themes, including those from Norse mythology. He believed that myths are a way for cultures to express these universal archetypes and that they serve as a bridge between the conscious and unconscious mind. The collective unconscious is a shared part of our psyche that holds these archetypal images and patterns. For instance, the hero's journey, seen in the tales of Sigurd and other Norse heroes, is a recurring motif representing personal growth and transformation. Jung argued that by studying these myths, we can gain insights into our psychological development and the universal patterns that shape our lives.

The therapeutic potential of Norse myths is vast. In modern therapy, these myths can help individuals explore their personal narratives and identities. By identifying with mythological characters and their stories, people can gain a deeper understanding of their own struggles and strengths. For example, someone facing a significant challenge might find inspiration in Thor's relentless battles against giants, drawing parallels to their own fight against adversity. Mythological symbols, such as Yggdrasil the World Tree, can also be used in Jungian analysis to represent the journey of self-discovery and the integration of different aspects of the self. These symbols provide a language to help people articulate complex emotions and experiences.

Norse mythology continues to be a valuable resource in both psychological theory and practice. Its rich collection of characters, symbols, and narratives offers insights into the human psyche and the universal patterns that shape our lives. By engaging with these ancient stories, we can gain a deeper understanding of ourselves and the world around us, finding new ways to navigate the complexities of modern life.

CONCLUSION

As we reach the end of our journey through the rich landscape of Norse mythology, it's time to reflect on the incredible stories and insights we've explored. We've examined the origins of the cosmos, witnessed the birth of gods and giants from the primordial void of Ginnungagap, and discovered the intricate realms of Yggdrasil, the World Tree. These myths have entertained us and offered deep lessons about the nature of existence and the human condition.

Throughout this book, we have met a pantheon of fascinating gods and goddesses, each with unique attributes and stories. Odin, with his relentless quest for wisdom, and Thor, the mighty protector of humankind, have shown us the value of knowledge and bravery. We've explored the dual nature of Loki, the trickster and catalyst of change, and felt the deep sorrow in the tale of Baldr's tragic death. These deities have woven a complex tapestry that reflects the values and anxieties of the Viking Age.

We've also walked alongside legendary heroes like Sigurd, who slew the dragon Fafnir, and Ragnar Lothbrok, whose exploits blend history and myth. Their stories of courage, cunning, and fate continue to inspire and resonate. The mythical creatures we've encountered, from the fearsome Fenrir to the wise and enigmatic dwarves, have enriched our understanding of the Norse cosmos, embodying the eternal struggle between order and chaos.

The rituals, symbols, and practices of the Norse people, such as the sacrificial Blót and the mystical Seidr, have given us a glimpse into their spiritual lives. These traditions, rooted in a deep connection to nature and the divine, reveal a holistic and cyclical worldview. The runes, with their magical and practical uses, and the solemnity of Viking funerals, paint a vivid picture of how the Norse honored life and death.

In exploring the modern impact of Norse mythology, we've seen how these ancient stories continue to shape contemporary literature, movies, TV shows, and even video games. The resurgence of Norse paganism and the influence of these myths in music and fashion highlight their enduring relevance. They offer a bridge between the past and the present, reminding us of the timeless nature of these narratives.

Writing this book has been a deeply personal journey for me. My passion for helping others understand and appreciate ancient traditions drove me to create this guide. Norse mythology, with its rich stories and profound lessons, has always fascinated me. I wanted to demystify it and make it accessible to everyone, regardless of their background. Sharing these tales and insights has been a labor of love, and I hope you've found it as rewarding to read as I have to write.

As we conclude, I encourage you to continue your exploration of Norse mythology. Let these stories inspire you to dive deeper into the myths and their cultural impact. Visit museums, read more books, and engage with communities that celebrate this rich heritage. The world of Norse mythology is vast and ever-evolving, with new interpretations and discoveries waiting to be uncovered.

Remember, these myths are more than just stories. They are reflections of human nature, mirrors of our hopes, fears, and dreams. They teach us the importance of bravery, wisdom, and accepting fate. They remind us that life is a journey filled with trials and triumphs and that every end is a new beginning.

Thank you for joining me on this journey. I hope this book has sparked a sense of wonder and curiosity in you. May the stories of the gods, heroes, and mythical creatures of Norse mythology stay with you, guiding and inspiring you in your own life's journey. Skål!

REFERENCES

"Barbarians and Literature - Viking Metal and Its Links to Old Norse Mythology." 2013. *Medievalists.Net* (blog). October 16, 2013. https://www.medievalists.net/2013/10/barbarians-and-literature-viking-metal-and-its-links-to-old-norse-mythology/.

"Brunhild in Norse Mythology | Origins, Significance & Facts." n.d. Study.Com. https://study.com/academy/lesson/brynhild-origins-mythology-norse.html.

"Egill Skallagrímsson | Viking Warrior, Saga Author." n.d. Britannica. https://www.britannica.com/biography/Egill-Skallagrimsson.

"Fafnir | Giant, Dragon, Hoarder." n.d. Britannica. https://www.britannica.com/topic/Fafnir.

"Fenrir | Giant Wolf, Norse God & Mythology." n.d. Britannica. https://www.britannica.com/topic/Fenrir.

"Frigg: Queen of Asgard, Beloved Norse Goddess, Mother." 2019. Ancient Origins: Reconstructing the Story of Humanity's Past. July 16, 2019. https://www.ancient-origins.net/myths-legends-europe/frigg-queen-asgard-beloved-norse-goddess-mother-009707.

"Ginnungagap | Norse Mythology." n.d. Britannica. https://www.britannica.com/topic/Ginnungagap.

"Greek and Norse Mythology: A Comparison." 2016. *The Avant Guardian* (blog). August 14, 2016. https://avantguardianblog.wordpress.com/2016/08/14/greek-and-norse-mythology-a-comparison/.

Greenberg, Mike. 2020. "Odin's Discovery of the Runes: The True Story." November 9, 2020. https://mythologysource.com/odins-discovery-of-the-runes/.

Hallahan, Sam. 2022. "God Of War Ragnarok Vs. Assassin's Creed Valhalla: Which Game Does Norse Better?" TheGamer. November 27, 2022. https://www.thegamer.com/god-of-war-ragnarok-vs-assassins-creed-valhalla-norse-mythology-comparison/.

Idrisoglu, Fatima Ali. 2022. "The Best TV Shows & Movies About Norse Mythology." MovieWeb. November 30, 2022. https://movieweb.com/norse-mythology-best-tv-and-movies/.

"Iðunn." 2024. In *Wikipedia*. https://en.wikipedia.org/w/index.php?title=I%C3%B0unn&oldid=1233497454.

Larkin, Josh. 2020. "Norse Mythology in Fantasy, Games and Culture." *Home of*

(Eventual) Author Josh Larkin (blog). February 16, 2020. https://writerlarkin. com/2020/02/16/norse-mythology-in-fantasy-games-and-culture/.

Mark, Joshua J. n.d.-a. "Jörmungandr." World History Encyclopedia. https://www. worldhistory.org/Jormungandr/.

———. n.d.-b. "Valkyrie." World History Encyclopedia. https://www.worldhisto ry.org/Valkyrie/.

———. n.d.-c. "Vikings." World History Encyclopedia. https://www.worldhisto ry.org/Vikings/.

"Norse Mythology: The Dwarves and Elves, Creators of Enchanted Artifact." 2024. Planderful Shop. September 1, 2024. https://www.planderful.com/blogs/ viking-treasures/norse-mythology-the-dwarves-and-elves-creators-of-enchanted-artifacts.

"Norse vs Celtic Mythology: Unraveling the Threads of Ancient Lore." 2023. *Viking Spirituality* (blog). November 7, 2023. https://vikingspirituality.com/ 2023/11/07/norse-vs-celtic-mythology-unraveling-the-threads-of-ancient-lore/.

"Odin: The Supreme Norse God of Wisdom, War and Magic." n.d. GreekMythology.Com. https://www. greekmythology.com/Myths/Norse/Odin/odin.html.

"Ragnar Lothbrok | Biography, Sons, Death, Vikings, & Facts." 2024. Britannica. September 9, 2024. https://www.britannica.com/topic/Ragnar-Lothbrok.

"Ragnarök | Gods, Giants & Monsters." n.d. Britannica. https://www.britannica. com/event/Ragnarok.

Scott, Jess. 2021. "Loki: The Story of the Trickster God." Life in Norway. January 11, 2021. https://www.lifeinnorway.net/loki-norse-mythology/.

"Seidr | Exploring Norse Magic, Shamanism and Divination." 2023. Vikingr. April 16, 2023. https://vikingr.org/magic-symbols/seidr.

Shelley, Andrea. 2023. "Futhark Runes: Symbols, Meanings and How to Use Them." Andrea Shelley Designs. January 9, 2023. https://andreashelley.com/ blog/futhark-runes-symbols-and-meanings/.

Suess, Jessica. 2024. "How Norse Mythology Inspired Tolkien's Lord of the Rings." TheCollector. June 12, 2024. https://www.thecollector.com/norse-mythology-lord-rings-tolkien/.

"The Binding of Fenrir." n.d. *Norse Mythology for Smart People* (blog). https://norse-mythology.org/tales/the-binding-of-fenrir/.

"The Creation Myth of Norse Mythology (The Nine Realms)." 2022. Vikingr. January 21, 2022. https://vikingr.org/norse-cosmology/norse-creation-myth.

"The Mead of Poetry." n.d. *Norse Mythology for Smart People* (blog). https://norse-mythology.org/tales/the-mead-of-poetry/.

"The Viking Blót Sacrifices." n.d. National Museum of Denmark. https://en.

natmus.dk/historical-knowledge/denmark/prehistoric-period-until-1050-ad/the-viking-age/religion-magic-death-and-rituals/the-viking-blot-sacrifices/.

"Thor's Hammer." n.d. *Norse Mythology for Smart People* (blog). https://norse-mythology.org/symbols/thors-hammer/.

"Yggdrasill | World Tree, Nine Realms, Norse Gods." 2024. Britannica. August 12, 2024. https://www.britannica.com/topic/Yggdrasill.